TONY MACAULAY is an author, broadcaster, peacebuilder, leadership consultant and suicide prevention advocate from Northern Ireland. He has spent over 30 years working to build peace and reconciliation at home and abroad. In 2008 he published a discussion paper proposing a five phase process for the removal of peace walls in Northern Ireland.

His debut critically acclaimed memoir *Paperboy* (2010) reflected on his experiences growing up in Belfast during the Troubles and in 2018 was turned into a hit musical by Andrew Doyle & Duke Special. Following the international success of *Paperboy* he wrote two further 'coming of age' memoirs, *Breadboy* (2013) and *All Growed Up* (2014). His fourth book *Little House on the Peace Line* (2017) tells the story of how he and his wife Lesley lived and worked on the peace line in Belfast in the 1980s.

This year Ulster University awarded him an honorary doctorate for services to literature and peace building at home and abroad.

G000244921

BELFAST GATE

Tony Macaulay

so-it-is

Introduction

A magpie alights on the old wall and surveys the empty streets below. She seeks an opening along the brow of the great barrier and pecks hungrily at any tiny gap.

Thirty feet below the street is silent; it's too early for bustle.

Suddenly she raises her beak, alert to a distant sound, an approaching vibration. Instinctively she ceases her search for insects. Now is a time for vigilance. The bird scans the streets below with a suspicious eye, fearing an imminent threat. She turns her head and twitches.

Life springs from one of the red-bricked side streets, rupturing the peace. The startled magpie jumps and flaps extended wings to restore balance.

'Bastards!' shouts a young man at the top of his voice.

The magpie freezes and stares down at the possible predator, unaware that a mere bird is not the target of his aggression. The attacker runs faster and faster towards the wall.

'Bastards!' he shouts again and again.

The magpie flaps in a panicky dance across the crest of the wall.

As the aggressor gathers momentum he meets no resistance down below. The rain-soaked streets remain deserted. Crying with fury the young man begins to raise the weapon in his hands.

'BASTARDS!' he screams violently, spying his target.

The magpie shits and flees. She leaves a streak of insulting white excrement along the face of the wall.

1

Six months earlier in a street in West Belfast a small woman is weeping. This is a place where many small women have wept before.

'She was the best friend I ever had, so she was,' cries Jean. 'A good neighbour for over forty years.'

A modest assembly of pensioners is standing shoulder to shoulder with Jean Beattie in front of a two-up two-down beside the peace wall. Known to her friends as Wee Jean, she has the sort of face people trust. Everyone says she has lovely skin, like the Queen.

'Poor Isobel,' says Roberta. 'She made the best caramel squares in Ulster.'

The women respond with knowing nods and share sad smiles in the drizzle.

'And her flies' graveyards were to die for,' adds Roberta.

Given the circumstances this comment elicits fewer nods.

'God love her,' weeps Patricia. 'Sure, she was cursed with weight all her life, same as you Jean, love, but not as bad as you Roberta, love.'

Jean gives Patricia a dirty look and flicks a wisp of pure white hair, while the mourners nod again and sniffle into an assortment of crumpled coloured tissues.

'And that oul blood pressure of hers,' says Roberta.

'I know Roberta, love,' says Patricia, 'it's been sky-high since before the ceasefires.'

Silence falls as a budget coffin emerges from Isobel Surgeoner's house, held high by two elderly men at the front and two younger undertakers at the back.

'God love her,' whispers Jean, 'she'd no men left belongin' to her to do a lift.'

A distressed Jack Russell terrier runs out the front door of Isobel's house and leaps up onto Patricia's lap. He is mainly white with two poorly defined brown patches on his back and mottled grey whiskers. The dog is wearing a plastic collar in biscuit-tin tartan. The Jack Russell nestles into Patricia's lap as if he has found a permanent haven. Patricia sniffs the reassuring dog smell on his coat.

'Don't you worry, Wee Jack Surgeoner,' she says, stroking the bereaved pet.

Dogs take on the surnames of their owners in Belfast so that neighbours can distinguish between Jack Russell terriers. Even the dogs in the street know that.

'You're the beautifulest wee dog I've ever seen in all my born days and you can come and live with me nigh your mammy's gone up to the happy huntin' ground.'

Wee Jack looks up with the widest of eyes, whimpers and snuggles his nose into Patricia's lap. She retrieves a large pink smartphone from beneath the cushion of her wheelchair and takes a photo of the dog.

'Patricia, will you have some respect and put that phone away, for God's sake!' says Jean. 'It's a funeral not a bloody weddin'.'

'I'm just taking a photie of Wee Jack for my Instergram, Jean. Isobel wouldn't have minded. She loved her Wee Jack, didn't she, son?' she says, snuggling her wet nose into the little dog's wet nose. 'You leave me alone, Jean, will ye?'

Jean and Roberta exchange glances and roll their eyes. 'Nightmare,' says Roberta.

The sombre black suits of Bilton's undertakers contrast with Jean's pink umbrella, Roberta's yellow anorak and Patricia's purple hair. The men stop beside a single black hearse and await further instructions. While most of the women bow their heads, Jean is becoming increasingly distracted. She repeatedly checks her mobile in case she has missed the vital call. A tall, tidy and distinguished-looking woman in a long black raincoat emerges from the back of the group and bends down to whisper in Jean's ear.

'Have they never phoned you back yet, Jean?'

'No, Bridget, love, indeed they have not.'

'Well, they're leavin' it very late, so they are,' interjects Patricia, prompting a disapproving shush from Bridget.

'They promised me they would open it for her. They promised!' whispers Jean. 'Don't worry. They're just very busy these days with all the wee hoods and joyriders and drugs and all.'

'I know, love,' says Bridget patting Jean on the shoulder, hoping to reassure her.

Jean takes her old friend's arm and shuffles Bridget past Patricia's wheelchair to stand slightly apart from the clatter of mourners. She knows she can rely on Bridget for a bit of common sense.

'Bridget, love, you know I promised Big Isobel that if she went before me, I would get it opened for her funeral.'

'I know, love,' says Bridget. 'Don't you be worrying now. It'll be alright.'

The two old friends look up at the thirty-foot-high wall in front of them and over towards the steeple of the small church on the other side. On top of the wall sits a single magpie surveying the scene below as attentively as the CCTV cameras along the peace line.

Protestants like Jean and Roberta live on this side and Catholics like Bridget and Patricia live on the other side. This barrier has separated these neighbours for more than fifty years now. Only the most elderly residents can remember a time when Catholics and Protestants lived together here in integrated streets between the Falls Road and the Shankill Road. Younger residents find this so unbelievable that they assume such reminiscences are a possible symptom of dementia.

As the homely huddle waits for news the women comfort one another with an occasional hug, a quiet pat on the arm and a friendly wipe of smudged mascara from a wrinkled cheek. As the minutes pass by, the stalled undertakers are beginning to struggle with the dead weight of the faux mahogany box. Bilton's men know how to handle a coffin but there are limits to how long even four experienced casket carriers can hold such a heavy burden aloft. Jean shakes her head at the slight wobbling of the coffin. Her typical tight perm remains unmoved but her irritation is increasing. Patricia starts to take a series of photographs of the scene, as if she is the appointed photojournalist for the occasion.

'Patricia, I'm warning you, if you take one more photo, I'll smash that friggin' mobile over your scone!'

'Don't you talk to me like that, Jean Beattie,' says Patricia, 'and our Isobel up there in her coffin listenin' on her funeral day and all. This is bloody ridiculous, so it is. I'm takin' as many photies as I want and I'm gonna send them all till Stephen Nolan at the BBC!'

'*Congratulations and jubilations, I want the world to know I'm happy as can be ...*'

Jean's ringtone cuts through the sombre mood. She squints down at the screen, recognises the caller's number and answers in her most polite Gloria Hunniford telephone voice. 'Hello? Yes. Good morning, chief inspector, thank you very much. We're all standing here in the rain soakin' and waitin'...'

Jean listens carefully to the response on the phone and gasps. Her bright blue eyes flash with anger. 'What do you mean youse can't open the gate?'

She is no longer adopting her polite telephone voice.

'Youse promised me you would get Isobel through the peace

gate to her wee church for the funeral. It's only two minutes round the corner!'

The faint sound of a stammering police officer can be heard coming from the earpiece of Jean's phone.

'Listen, love, I don't want to hear about scarce resources and don't even talk to me about health and bloody safety. There's a crowd of senior citizens standing here in the rain like Brown's cows waitin' for youse to do your job and open this gate. I want my friend to get to her own funeral!'

A murmur of disapproval spreads among the mourners. Jean puts a forefinger in her free ear so she can hear exactly what is being said. Patricia's pencil-drawn eyebrows arch even more steeply than usual and she manoeuvres her electric wheelchair forwards so that her voice projects into the mouthpiece of Jean's phone.

'Blinkin' disgrace!' she shouts.

'Shush, Patricia!' chides Bridget as Jean begins to speak again.

'What do you mean *security considerations*? All the wee hoods are still in bed! There's only a clatter of oul dolls down here, from both sides, and we're not fightin' with nobody!'

As she listens to an unsatisfactory explanation Jean begins to rub at the spot where her neck meets her upper chest. It feels soft, hot and tender.

Roberta notices this with some concern. 'Oh, here, I'm worried about her,' she whispers to Bridget. 'Wee Jean's had trouble with her vangina for years.'

'*An*gina, Roberta, *an*gina!' says Bridget, digging Roberta with her elbow.

At sixty-eight years old Roberta is the youngest of the group of friends. She is the shortest and plumpest and is prone to malapropisms at the most inappropriate moments. Today the rain is causing her fake tan to run down her neck.

'Look at the cut of you, Roberta, with that orange tan,' says Patricia. 'You look like Donald friggin' Trump meltin'. When are you gonna realise you're just as lovely without it, love?'

'It's because I'm worth it, so I am,' replies Roberta with a flick of her hair and all the confidence of a L'Oréal model.

The undertakers, still awaiting further instructions, are now sweating and trying to retain some level of dignity and decorum. Net curtains twitch in the windows of the red-bricked terraced houses on either side of the street. At the front of the coffin, William Senior and Mervyn Senior glance back to see how Young William and Young Mervyn are coping at the rear. It usually takes six men to lift a coffin of this weight, so the undertakers are going well beyond the call of duty.

Jean places her forefinger to her lips to hush the other women. 'Are you takin' the hand out of me, chief inspector?' she asks. 'There's hardly gonna be much of a riot on the interface this mornin'! There's only ten oul weemin here. And one of them's dead!' She stabs the red button on her phone and begins to sob into her tissue, which disintegrates and falls like soggy confetti onto the puddled pavement. It's not a self-pitying sob. It's a cry of sincere regret.

Bridget places a comforting hand on Jean's shoulder. 'Och, Jean, this is awful.'

'I'm bloody ragin', Bridget. I promised her!' Then after a short, thoughtful pause she adds, 'We're gonna have to do somethin' about this!'

'We will, love, we will,' replies Bridget, even though she has no idea how to do anything about it.

Then with an uncertain nod from Jean, the soaked and perspiring fathers and sons of Bilton's Funeral Directors carry the coffin towards the pedestrian opening beside the peace gate. The huge steel gate across the road is firmly locked, bolted and chained shut and the small steel doorway is the only way through the barrier at the end of the street.

The peace wall was built in 1969 to separate working-class Protestants and Catholics in a city at war with itself. Back then neighbours were burning each other's homes down but nothing on this scale has happened since the 1970s. Today the huge structure protects wary residents from bored children throwing stones at an unknown enemy. The Troubles have been over for decades now, but the peace wall remains intact. No vehicle has passed through this barrier for decades. The direct route to Isobel's church, just around the corner, is blocked off, as it has been for fifty years.

This upset won't make the news today – most people living in Belfast don't really care. A mile away in the city centre shoppers sipping on cappuccinos have no interest in the everyday challenges of life on the peace line. The Troubles are a distant memory, far removed from them, in impact or responsibility.

Many years ago the construction of this section of the peace wall left a lonely Methodist church on the Catholic side of the peace line, hastening the decline of its Protestant congregation. Nevertheless, Isobel Surgeoner was there every Sunday morning, through it all, in her good coat, white gloves and best shoes, until the very end.

Undeterred, the mourners follow the coffin towards the pedestrian opening, taking down their umbrellas as they walk. The women know from bitter experience that the spokes of umbrellas have a habit of getting stuck in the railings of the narrow pedestrian passage in the peace wall, which is a terrible nuisance because it rains on both sides of the community. Jean turns to the shuffling mourners and with a defiant wave of her retracted umbrella she makes a proclamation.

'Remember this, girls. If it's the last thing I do, I'll make sure this bloody gate's away for *my* funeral.'

'Yeoooo!' shouts Roberta with a thumbs up. 'You tell them, Jean, ya girl ye!'

The four undertakers are starting to struggle as they stop short of the gap in the wall and the mourners take their appointed places behind the coffin. This is familiar territory for the widows, mothers and daughters of West Belfast. They have mourned together and apart, through bad days and worse days, many times before. On these streets they have protested against each other, rallied together for peace and walked behind hearses containing the coffins of friends and family lost to the Troubles. Jean, Roberta, Patricia and Bridget are the chief mourners and the other few women, in a collection of plastic headscarves and raincoats, shuffle into the procession behind them. Patricia nods insistently towards William Senior in the direction of the pedestrian opening but he hesitates. Young William and Young Mervyn are wobbling more noticeably now under the sustained strain of the large casket. Big Isobel did indeed adore her tray bakes.

'She always said she wanted to be driven around the corner for her last wee service,' says Jean, 'in a big black hearse from Bilton's, dead slow, like, with us all walkin' behind her—'

'Aye, like, Geordie Best up till Stormount!' says Roberta, her small, thick bottle-top glasses now steamed up with the heat of emotion.

A further flurry of nods spreads among the mourners and Patricia continues to take photographs of the scene, ignoring disapproving glares from Bridget and Jean.

'I'm sending these till Nolan! I'm tellin' ye!' she shouts.

The two senior undertakers try to work out how to manoeuvre the heavy coffin through such a confined space.

'Don't worry, love. We should be able to squeeze her through here,' says Jean, ever the optimist.

In the past, the Bilton brothers coped with all sorts of challenging funeral scenarios: they dealt with the demands of the paramilitary funeral – flags, balaclavas and shots over the coffin; they managed their way through the sensitivities of a multitude of inappropriate floral displays and musical accompaniments; and they coped with the increasing strains of obesity – but this is new territory. The women huddle together, arm in arm in the rain during this uncertain pause in the procession.

'What did the peelers say, Jean?' asks Patricia.

'They said it's not in the interests of public safety to open the gate because all them wee lads have been *recreational* riotin'.'

'What's "erectional" riotin' anyway, Jean?' asks Roberta.

Jean's eyes narrow as she answers. She's never quite sure how deliberate Roberta's mispronunciations are. '*Recreational* riotin' is wee scumbegs textin' each other, across the wall, to come down here for a sectarian fight to throw stones outside MY house!'

Jean's house is at the end of the terrace, nestling against the peace wall.

'Flip me, Jean!' says Patricia, 'in my day you didn't need a mobile to start a riot. I just spat at a wee angry Prod or kicked a Brit, when I had my legs, like.'

'Sure, those wee lads don't even remember the Troubles,' adds Bridget.

'They're wee hoods with nathin' better to do, Bridget. And our side's as bad as their side,' says Patricia.

The Biltons continue with their valiant attempt to carry the coffin through the narrow gap in the peace wall. They try it one way, then another, but no matter how many ways they angle the coffin, or pull it or push it, the casket will not squeeze through the limited space available.

'Look, them four pockles will never get our Isobel through thon gate,' whispers Jean.

During the course of one attempt, Young William crushes his thumb against the gate hinge and emits a quiet and disbelieving 'Fuck!' William Senior is clearly horrified but Young Mervyn stifles a smile.

'Oh, my God!' cries Roberta, suddenly realising the scale of the problem. 'Nightmare! Big Isobel's gonna get stuck in the peace wall!'

The undertakers are now red-faced, injured and sweating. As the mourners look on with an increasing look of distaste on their faces, the funeral directors realise their attempts to maintain sombre decorum are doomed. Wee Jack Surgeoner sniffs and blinks repeatedly, standing up and sitting down on Patricia's lap in synchronicity with every move of the casket, as if supervising the progress of his owner's final journey.

Jean shakes her head again and again. 'I don't believe this. I don't believe this,' she says.

'Jesus, Mary and Joseph,' says Patricia, 'she'll never see the inside of Roselawn crematorium the day!'

'Oh, my God,' shrieks Roberta, 'them fumical directors are goin' till coup!'

Finally William Senior shakes his head to confirm the impossibility of the task. He leads an about-turn and attempts to regain some dignity as the funeral procession reverses back towards the hearse parked outside Isobel's house. The attempted route has been a failure and everyone is aware of the possible riotous consequences of a rerouted procession in these streets. On this occasion there is no outbreak of violence but Jean can feel within her chest a growing pulse of anger and determination. Her frustration breaks the silence.

'It's a bloody disgrace!' she exclaims. 'Now they have to drive the poor crater halfway round Belfast just to get her to her own wee church around the corner!'

Wee Jack yelps in frustration as the forlorn mourners trudge back towards Isobel's empty house, in the rain, with a look of resignation on their faces.

Patricia has had enough, and looking heavenward to the grey skies she shouts, 'This is supposed to be a funeral. Not the hokey-bloody-cokey!'

Jean places a hand on the coffin and whispers through cold, wet wood. 'Don't you worry, Isobel, love. I promise you, I'm gonna do somethin' about this.'

2

By the time Jean and Roberta re-emerge through the pedestrian opening in the peace gate, the mountain overlooking West Belfast has returned to its usual black hue. Jean is walking briskly and even though Roberta is fifteen years younger, she is playing catch-up, a few paces behind her dear friend. It's been a long, sad and exhausting day.

'Ach, Jean, I broke my heart when Daniel started singin'. It was beautiful, so it was.'

'I just hope we done her proud, Roberta.'

'Do you remember the time she made five hundurd tray bakes for the street party for the Royal Jubilee?'

'Aye, there were more caramel squares than Union Jacks that day!'

The women are so engrossed in recounting happy memories of Isobel that they fail to notice two teenage boys painting sectarian graffiti on the Protestant side of the gate. With a shaven head, broken nose and sad eyes, Sam Spence looks like he has lived much longer than his eighteen years. The drugs and the sectarian fights on the interface have taken a toll. He has a distinctive scar on the dimple of his chin from a skirmish when he fought to keep these streets British. His millimetre fringe, gelled forwards determinedly, and his grey tracksuit are the only evidence of style consciousness. Beside him, as always, is his small, thin friend, Lee Campbell, whose long floppy hair and oversized Man United football shirt make him look younger than his fifteen years. The boys are painting words that generations of Protestant teenagers have inflicted on similar walls to express their loyalty to the British Crown: *Kill All Taigs* and *Fuck the Pope*. Jean and Roberta are too busy reviewing their day of mourning to notice the vandalism.

'At least we gave her the best send-off we could. Sure, the church service was lovely and now she's goin' to be planted under a wee tree at Roselawn,' says Jean.

'Aye, that's right, Jean, love. Big Isobel always said she wanted to go down into that there big oven with Daniel O'Donnell doin' "How Great Thou Art".'

'Aye, it was lovely, so it was.'

'And all her wee friends from over there on the other side were at the cematorium too,' adds Roberta, highlighting the great significance of Isobel's Catholic friends from across the peace wall attending a Protestant funeral.

'Sure, people can't be bothered with all that oul them-and-us nonsense nighadays,' says Jean.

'I know, Jean. Sure, we're supposed to have peace nigh. But c'mere till I tell ye, them gabshites up at Stormount haven't a notion. Sure, we haven't had a bloody government in yonks and that shower up there don't give a monkey's if this hateful wall never comes down.'

Lee notices the two women have come from the wrong side of the peace wall. Recognising Jean and Roberta as neighbours from his street, he is instantly unimpressed. Going over to the other side is an act of disloyalty, even for old women. Impulsively he decides to challenge this appeasement of republican plans to dominate his community and eradicate his culture. This is also a good opportunity to impress Sam, so he approaches the two pensioners with all the aggression he can muster. Lee stands defiantly, square in front of the two women, even though he is slightly shorter and considerably thinner than both. Neither woman notice him at first until he spits aggressively on the pavement in front of them.

'Have you got the cold, love?' enquires Roberta.

Lee places his hands on his slight hips.

'What do yousens think youse were doin' over there?' he shouts, accentuating his question with a further catarrh-laden spit.

Jean and Roberta halt where Lee has blocked their path. The two women look at him with a mix of motherly sympathy and indignation. Then, in perfect unison, Jean and Roberta also place their hands on their hips.

'No, wee son! What do yousens think youse are doing right *here*?' asks Jean, pointing emphatically towards her feet as if she owns the very tarmac on the street.

Sam turns his head slightly but does not look directly at the women. That would be giving them too much undeserved acknowledgement. 'None of your fuckin' business,' he says snorting.

'Aye!' shouts Lee, emboldened by Sam backing him up.

Lee first experienced the excitement of sectarian tensions when his father brought him along to some of the flag protests while he was still at primary school. It was an adventure, and Lee discovered that if you felt angry about someone taking your flag down, you could block the main road and set cars on fire and no one would try to stop you.

'Don't you dare swear at Wee Jean,' says Roberta. 'Were you dragged up?'

'None of your fuckin' business,' says Lee, trying to sound as hard as Sam.

Jean gasps, takes a step back and then points at her house beside the peace gate. 'It *is* my business, wee fella,' she asserts. 'I live here!' She rubs her neck. 'I've to look out my windies at that mess you're makin' every day, son, so less of your oul lip!'

'Aye, less of your oul slabberin', ya cheeky wee glipe!' joins in Roberta. 'That woman's just come from buryin' her best friend!'

Lee draws close to Roberta, so close she can smell an

aromatic mix of cigarettes, chewing gum and Lynx body spray. He points his dripping blue paintbrush at Roberta as if it is a loaded weapon. 'Fuck! Off!' he barks into Roberta's face. Lee once again spits aggressively as he knows this intimidates and disgusts women in particular. His mother always gave him a good hiding for spitting.

Jean is not standing for this impudence and pushes the slight teenager out of Roberta's way.

'You watch your language, wee lad, or I'll give you a good clip round the ear!'

Sam stifles a chuckle as Lee steadies himself. Lee's cheeks redden at Sam's disrespect and he looks around the street to check if anyone else has observed this humiliation. For Lee, the only thing more important than being a hardman is to be seen to be a hardman, especially by bigger lads like Sam.

'Should you not be at home doin' your homework, wee lad?' asks Roberta.

Sam turns around for the first time to give the incident his full attention. 'Sure, they threw him out of school for settin' the library on fire,' he says, simultaneously mocking Lee and the two women.

'But they took the tyres off our boney!' shouts Lee indignantly.

'So you tried to burn your own school down. Are you as thick as champ or what, wee lad?' replies Roberta.

Lee kicks the kerb, stubbing his big toe in the process, and stifles a painful 'Fuck!'

'She used to work there, ya know,' says Roberta.

'Where?' asks Sam.

'Wee Jean was the school dinner lady for forty years, so she was.'

Lee spits again defiantly. His mouth is now dry. He knows he is running out of effective spittle. Fearful of losing face in front of Sam he turns his back on the women, returning his focus to his graffiti craft. 'Well, I bet your fish fingers were mingin', missus,' he says, as if the two women are now invisible.

Jean turns her attention to the older boy. She looks closely at Sam's face, recognising him. 'Here, are you not big William Spence's son? Big William from down the Road?' she asks.

'Oh, aye, yer man the boxer. He's a lovely big man,' adds Roberta, softer now. 'He goes to all the wee meetin's at the mission hall and he's a quare good preacher and all.'

Roberta goes to the wee meetin's in the mission hall on a Sunday night, especially if she's feeling lonely and *I'm a Celebrity ... Get Me Out of Here!* is not on UTV. She admires William Spence's preaching of the Gospel. He always manages to make hell sound particularly horrifying when he tells you that you're going there. Roberta regards William Spence as one of the few old-fashioned Orangemen left because he still reads the Bible and doesn't drink Carlsberg Special at the parades.

However, the mention of his father produces an unexpected response from Sam. He rolls his eyes in disgust at his praise. William threw Sam out of the house two months ago. He said he'd had enough of his prodigal son with his drugs and his joyriding. Sam slept on Lee's sister's couch until he got a tiny bedsit on housing benefit, above the bookies, with a bed and a fridge. Sam's mother wept for a week and secretly sent him boxes of scones and a supply of the chocolate digestive biscuits he liked to dunk in his tea when he was a wee boy. But it was too late. Sam would never return home now.

He turns around and for the first time comes face-to-face with the two women. Gesticulating with a red paintbrush in his hand he decides to engage with these two annoying oul dolls. 'Aye, so what if I'm the fuckin' Pope's son?' he asks angrily.

'Love, I don't think the Pope has a son, so he doesn't,' says Roberta. 'Is he not supposed to be, like, you know ... celebrate and a virgin and all?'

'Aye, a virgin like you, Lee!' says Sam laughing.

Lee's cheeks redden at the ultimate put-down. To be called out for being a virgin as well as being likened to the leader of the Roman Catholic Church was a doubly devastating charge.

'Well, I thought your da was an awful good-livin' big man,' says Jean. 'He'll not like it if I tell him you're up to all this oul nonsense.'

'It's none of his fuckin' business neither!' retorts Sam, swiftly turning back to complete the last letter of the sectarian slogan.

Jean and Roberta look on in disbelief.

Very deliberately turning back to look straight at the two women, Sam hurls the remainder of the paint tin over his shoulder and over the top of the peace gate with savage belligerence. 'Fenian bastards!' he shouts, fixing his eyes defiantly on the two women.

Jean and Roberta jump with fright and rush towards Jean's front door. Even though the insult was not directed at them, the venom evident in the yell is chilling.

'Them wee lads scare me, Jean,' says Roberta, as Jean fumbles for her front door key. 'Where does all that hate come from? I thought we had peace nigh.'

'I don't know, Roberta,' replies Jean, inserting the key in the door with some relief. 'Maybe I'm livin' in cloud cuckoo land thinkin' we could ever get that blinkin' gate opened.'

As Jean and Roberta retreat into the safety of Jean's house, Lee feels a familiar urge to compete with and impress Sam. Lifting a conveniently located stray Belfast brick, he hurls it across the peace gate.

'No Surrender!' he roars.

He is throwing a red brick for Ulster. But this exertion is a little too much for Lee's slight frame, and he has to lean against the wall for a rest. He removes an asthma inhaler from his pocket, his eyes darting around the street to make sure no one is observing this temporary moment of weakness. Sam folds his arms and looks on, shaking his head. Lee is humiliated. Just once he would like to truly impress Sam, but it never works out that way.

It's been like this all Lee's life. He could see the fear and respect in the eyes of everyone who met his father, the big man on the Road, the much-feared brigadier in the UDA. His father had muscles and tattoos and could beat any man on the Road in a street fight. However, Lee had inherited his mother's slight frame and no matter how many steroid shakes he took, he could not add sufficient bulk to develop an intimidating frame like his infamous father. He wanted to be like Conor McGregor but in reality was more like Jedward. The more he tries to impress Sam, the more he fails, and Sam doesn't seem to give a damn. After a few final puffs of the inhaler, Lee finally gathers sufficient energy for one more manly but empty projectile of spittle against the peace wall.

'What are you like, wee lad?' says Sam laughing.

3

'I was never as glad in my life to get inside and into a workin' kitchen!' says Roberta.

'Sit down and calm yourself, love,' says Jean.

Roberta remains standing in the middle of the room. Jean's kitchen is clean and tidy but worn, dated and in need of repair. This most important room in the house is where she spends most of her time. She has an armchair in the corner and a not-so-flat TV that she insists will do her her day. The kitchen smells of freshly baked scones and recently bleached linoleum. On the plain white walls are elaborate gilt-framed pictures of her late husband Derek in the good suit she buried him in, and her son Trevor standing proudly at his graduation alongside his immaculately dressed and coiffured now-wife, Valerie. A framed snapshot of her well-built grandson, Darren, wearing his army uniform and sunglasses in Afghanistan, has pride of place in the centre of the wall just above a Cliff Richard calendar and a signed picture postcard of Julian Simmons from UTV. A newspaper puli-out souvenir picture-spread of Prince Harry and Meghan Markle's wedding day completes the montage of VIPs on the kitchen wall.

Roberta stares at the various pictures. 'Awk, Jean, I love all them beautiful pictures you put up on your wall of Harry and Meghan Marple.'

Jean nods.

'Oh, I'll never forget that wedding! They're a lovely couple, so they are, even if he is ginger, God love him, and her dress was gorgeous and that wee black preacher man from America was brilliant, wasn't he? Even if he did go on a bit preaching about love to all them toffee-nosed oul aristocats. Lady Di would have loved it! Did you see the look on all their bakes? Them royals looked like they'd just had a good suck of a lemon!'

Roberta is on a roll and once she gets started Jean knows there is no point in attempting an interruption.

'But, now, c'mere till I tell ye, Meghan's da seems a bit of an oul rip and my heart broke that Diana wasn't there to see her Harry on his big day, and to be honest with you, Jean, I'm still not sure about that Camilla, and did you see the bake on yer woman Posh Spice—'

'Roberta! I said sit down and calm yourself, love,' Jean finally interrupts.

She clicks on the kettle and Roberta takes her usual seat at the same clean Formica table where the pair have consumed an ocean of tea over the years, one milky cup at a time.

'I'll make you a nice cup-a-tay to calm your wee nerves, love,' says Jean, extracting a Battenberg cake from a cupboard with a squeaky broken door hinge.

'Aye, Jean, that'll be lovely,' answers Roberta. 'I'm scundered with them wee scumbegs out there. They're always standin' on the street corners drinkin' Buckfast and takin' drugs and callin' each other mammyfeckers across the wall! I don't understand them at all, so I don't.'

'They don't know any better,' says Jean. 'That wall was built before they were ever born and they can't even see the people on the other side, never mind meet them or make friends, like us. That's the world they were born into and they think it's normal.'

'No wonder so many young people are leavin' this place, especially all them millentials,' says Roberta.

Jean looks up and smiles at her precious family photographs.

'Well, guess what, Roberta? I think I've finally persuaded my Trevor to move back home, so I have,' she shares with a flurry of excitement in her voice as she serves the tea.

Jean reaches for her old 1970s Quality Street tin containing a multitude of tray bakes, but when she looks inside there's a sharp intake of breath and she begins to cry. Roberta stops mid sip with a look of confusion and concern. She has never seen Jean react in such a manner to any freshly baked product before.

'Turn the big light on, love!' cries Jean.

Roberta leaps up to switch the centre light on so it can illuminate the contents of the biscuit tin. Jean carries the receptacle to the kitchen table as if she has found rare treasure. She places her discovery before Roberta. Jean points gently at something within the tin and Roberta peeks inside tentatively.

'That must have been the last caramel square Big Isobel ever made,' weeps Jean.

'Dear God, I thought it was a mouse or a turd or somethin'!' says Roberta.

Jean sits on her armchair in front of Roberta and wipes the tears from her eyes with today's paper tissue, retrieved from its usual resting place in her knitted blue cardigan cuff.

'Ach, stop you upsettin' yourself, love,' says Roberta. 'We're gonna make sure everyone round here remembers Big Isobel. Do you mind the time she made Irish stew for all the pensioners in a big pot over a bonfire in her backyard during the Ulster Workers' Strike and all, and when the paramilitaries came and accused her of breakin' the strike she told them to frig away off? She was always—'

Jean's landline interrupts the latest memory. She picks up the handset of the jade faux marble telephone from Argos Trevor had bought her for Christmas the first year he moved away from home.

'Hello …' she says, and then mouths proudly to Roberta, 'it's my big son in England.'

Roberta nods and smiles to acknowledge the importance of the call, shuffles forwards in her chair and listens intently to every word crackling out of the swanky earpiece.

'Well, how's your Valerie's migraines, Trevor, love? ... Ah, that's good, son. Just let her lie in the dark whenever she needs it, love. Any word from our wee Darren in Afghanistan?' Jean stands up. 'Oh, that's good. So he'll be home soon? He sent me a lovely photograph. I'm so proud of him, but I wish he was home safe and sound, and he needs to put on a wee bit of weight again with some good home cookin'.' She looks up, smiling proudly at the picture of her grandson in his desert uniform, holding a gun and resting against a tank. 'Aye ... yes, son ... Big Isobel, God love her ... we're just back nigh ... The service was beautiful and she was lovely in her coffin and all, but they wouldn't open the peace gate for the funeral, you know, in case it started a riot. Would you believe the nonsense of that, love?'

Jean nods at Trevor's words and Roberta nods at Jean's nods at Trevor's words.

'But, sure, them wee hoods wouldn't have been riotin' in the mornin' anyway. Sure, they never get up before *Loose Women*, the lazy wee shites ... Anyway, son, have you and Valerie decided when yousens are movin' back home to Northern Ireland? I can't wait to have youse close to home again. What's the latest, love?'

Roberta notices a change in tone in the voice on the other end of the phone line. It sounds apologetic. Suddenly Jean has a look of terrible disappointment on her face.

'I know, son, but I miss youse terrible, so I do ... I know ... oh, I know, I know ... sure, think about it, won't you now? I'm sure Valerie will come round. Sure the air down in Bangor would be good for her headaches and her nerves and her chest and everything.'

Roberta notes another change of tone in the flurry of words now coming down the phone line. People who think Roberta is not the full shilling are often proved wrong. She can spot insincerity a mile off. Patricia says, 'Americans would call our Roberta a good bullshit detector even if her head is full of sweetie mice.'

'Alright, love. Tell your Valerie I was askin' for her. Bye-bye now, son. Bye, love. Bye-bye.'

Jean hangs up the telephone and gazes at the pictures of her family on the kitchen wall. Roberta notices a slight narrowing of Jean's eyes when she looks at Valerie's picture.

'You must be awful proud of them all,' says Roberta, sensing a need to support her friend. 'Your Trevor with a good job in the bank in England and wee Darren fightin' Ikea in Iraq.'

'It's the Taliban in Afghanistan, Roberta! Trevor says that's why they'll never move back here,' says Jean.

'Wha—because of the Talerbam?' asks Roberta.

'No! Them wee hoods out there riotin' and no government and them peace walls still up and all. He says this here place will never change. What are we gonna do, Roberta?'

Roberta knows this is not a time for words. She sets down her teacup, rises from the kitchen table and gives Jean a long, comforting hug.

4

The next day Jean is busily doing her front step. A perfectly bleached front step is a symbol of decency in Belfast and Jean is determined to remain fastidious in cleansing said step for as long as she has her health. Dressed in navy working slacks, matching polo-necked jumper and her favourite tartan apron, that Isobel brought her from her final holiday to Ayr, she is on her hands and knees vigorously bleaching and scrubbing the single doorstep at her front door.

Jean remembers the days when there wasn't a dirty step the whole length of the street – apart from Mrs Fletcher's step but her husband was one for the horses and women and poor Iris was bad with her knees and her nerves. Today only one in ten front steps in the street is totally bleached. Jean regards this as a symbol of the decline in civilisation in her lifetime. Well bleached steps rank high among leaving your front door open and polishing your brass letterbox, a feature of 'the good old days before microwaves, videos and the interwebs', as Roberta would say.

When the postman approaches he notices Jean doesn't look her usual cheerful self. That good oul crater's startin' to get on a bit now, he thinks, as Jean rubs her back and sighs while taking a break from determined step scrubbing.

As she looks up, to her great surprise who should be walking down the street, head down, texting on a recently unlocked stolen mobile phone, but Sam Spence, the graffiti artist from the previous night. Jean stands up to her full four feet ten inches, like a curious ageing meerkat.

'Here, wee lad,' she calls, 'I hope you're not comin' round here to cause more trouble!'

Sam stops beside Jean but continues texting until he is ready to acknowledge Jean's presence, just to make sure she knows who is in control. 'Wise up, missus. Nobody who riots gets up before *Loose Women*,' he says and begins to walk on.

'Houl yer horses, wee lad!' replies Jean, setting aside her red basin and worn scrubbing brush to give Sam her full attention.

Sam stops with an eye-roll and a smirk.

'How do you get each other's numbers?' asks Jean.

'Wha?'

'How do you know the mobile numbers of them wee lads over there on the other side of the peace wall? Sure, don't yousens text themuns for a riot?'

'Sure, we go out with wee girls from over there all the time – in the clubs, down the town,' he replies, softening slightly.

'Oh, so it's okay to do some things with the other side, then?' says Jean.

'Aye, Wee Jean, some things you leave religion out of,' says Sam laughing.

Jean continues to attempt engaging with the young man as he seems marginally less angry than yesterday. 'Why do you do it, love? I thought you were supposed to be a brilliant boxer like your da.'

Sam looks down, turns away slightly and puts his hood up, seeming vulnerable for a second. 'Aye, well, you thought wrong, didn't ye?' he huffs.

'Do you not have a job nor nathin'?' asks Jean.

'Nah'

'Why not, love? Sure, you've a good head on your shoulders, have you not?'

'Nah. Sure, I'm stupid.'

Jean walks forwards and places a hand on Sam's shoulder.

He looks straight at her for the first time and notices her very kind eyes.

'Who told you that? There's nathin' stupid about you, wee lad. Do you want to work? What are you good at?'

'Dunno ... well ... I'm good with cars, so I am—'

'Aye, he's good at joyridin', the wee scumbeg!' interrupts the postman, pulling down Sam's hood and clipping him round the ear. 'You're wastin' your time there, Jean,' he says. 'That wee lad needs nathin' but a good toe up the hole!'

Sam spits on the pavement. It is a full and wholehearted hackle. Spittle is an incisive means of expression for the angry young men of Belfast.

'Piss off, Postman Prat!' he snaps, his angry stance returning.

The postman gives Sam a threatening *just you try it, sunshine!* stare as he hands Jean an official-looking envelope.

Jean places the letter in her apron pocket as the postman shoves Sam aside and continues with his deliveries. Sam makes an obligatory obscene gesture in the direction of the departing postman and Jean picks up her scrubbing brush to continue bleaching her front step.

'Well, my Derek always said there was good in everyone,' she says.

'He never met me,' said Sam quietly to himself.

'I heard that. Don't be sayin' that, love.'

'Sure, I'm a wee scumbeg, isn't that what youse all call us?'

Jean looks up. 'If I needed a few wee jobs done round the house, son, could I trust you?' she asks.

'Why would you trust me? Sure, I'm scum,' he says, kicking at the painted kerbstones.

Jean stops scrubbing and looks up in shock. Sam walks off with his head down pulling his hood up once more. Jean stands up with her hands on her hips and looks after him, shaking her head.

Then she remembers the unexpected letter she has just received. It doesn't look like one of her usual bills or an appeal from Africa. She takes the letter from her apron pocket and opens it. As Jean stands on her damp doorstep reading the letter a look of astonishment breaks out on her face. She drops her scrubbing brush into the basin, with a splash so sudden that a passing mongrel, Patch McCormick, yelps and runs away. Jean rereads the letter, aloud this time, as if doing so will help her absorb the import of the words therein.

'Dear Mrs Beattie, in the matter of the estate of Isobel Surgeoner I have pleasure in informing you that in her last will and testament the said Mrs Surgeoner has bequeathed to you a legacy of three thousand pounds.'

Jean has a sharp intake of breath and holds her chest, panting, 'Oh, my God!' She continues to read aloud, although no one else in the street is listening apart from the magpie shitting on top of the peace gate. 'This gift is left to you on the condition that you use the money as Mrs Surgeoner stated in her will: to do up your working kitchen.'

'Oh, my God!'

Jean drops the letter in disbelief.

'Oh, my God!'

'Oh, Derek, love!'

'Oh, my God!'

The letter falls into the basin. Jean shrieks and quickly retrieves it, drying it on her apron, inspecting it again and again to make sure no lasting smudging has been caused. Once she is certain the document is intact and the whole incident is not a dream, she smiles, clutches the letter to her chest and runs inside.

5

'My head's turned with this oul weather of ours,' says Jean.

'Nightmare!' says Roberta. 'Sure, it never stops except when the sun comes out.'

It's one week later and it is still raining. This is Belfast, where it rains on even more days than they hold elections – when the loyal population returns the same Orange and Green politicians every time and then complains about them as much as the weather.

Once again Jean and Roberta are crossing the divide in their community as they shuffle through the pedestrian opening in the peace gate, arriving on the other side of the wall where their Catholic friends and neighbours live. Barbed wire rests on top of the peace wall even though none of the pensioners, or anyone else living there, has ever attempted to climb over the top.

Roberta is imagining the peace wall is like one of those force fields in a science fiction B-movie she went to see in the Stadium Cinema on the Shankill Road in the 1960s. She imagines she is a space warrior woman with silver skin wearing a Bacofoil dress crossing an invisible barrier to a dangerous parallel universe on the other side. But the daydream is broken when she stands in dog's dirt that covers the pavement on the other side too.

'Bloody dogs! Bloody council! Bloody country!' she says.

Roberta and Jean remember when this had been a mixed area, where Catholics and Protestants lived next door to each other, before the start of the Troubles when residents got burnt-out to create homogenous zones. The women knew more of the people who got burnt-out than those who did the burning, or maybe nobody talked about that any more. At the cross-community pensioners' club the women often reminisce about the good old days when everyone in your street didn't have to be the same religion, vote for the same political party and when you didn't have to have an identical culture.

'Sure, I remember before the Troubles all the Catholics used to come out and watch the parades on the Twelfth of July, and they loved it!' Roberta would say.

'Well, now, I wouldn't say that,' Patricia would reply.

'Well, okay, Patricia, I know there was discrimination against Catholics for houses and jobs and all,' Jean would comment, 'but we were just as poor as yousens, ya know.'

'I bet we were poorer than you!' says Patricia. 'I had to collect potato skins for pocket money.'

'Well, I was poorer than all of youse. I got my Christmas presents from Doctor Barnardo!' says Roberta.

The cross-community pensioners don't agree about everything in the past but all agree that they want a better future.

Today Jean and Roberta are wearing their favourite transparent plastic headscarves to protect their most recent perms, and they are sharing a similarly transparent plastic umbrella. Roberta holds the umbrella with one hand while applying a shocking pink lipstick with the other hand. Jean is carrying a tin of tray bakes in one hand while clutching in the other hand, in her good raincoat pocket, the precious envelope containing the letter from Isobel's solicitor. Suddenly the two women stop, noticing an all too familiar scene at the peace gate.

'I don't believe this, Roberta!' exclaims Jean.

On the Catholic side of the peace wall another two young men are painting sectarian graffiti on the gate.

'Oh, I know, love, I think I'm having a big déjà view!' says Roberta.

It's a mirror image of the scene Jean and Roberta observed the previous week on their own side of the wall – only the words are different. On this side the graffiti says *Kill All Prods* as opposed to last week's *Kill All Taigs*. The dissimilarity in the graffiti art are the colour of paint and the target of the intended genocide. On this side of the peace wall the admonishment to murder is brightened with orange and green as opposed to red and blue. The only shared shade is shroud white.

Anto notices that two wee Prods have ventured through the pedestrian opening onto his territory. He stops painting graffiti, turns around, walks towards Jean and Roberta in an intimidating manner and points his dripping green paintbrush at the two women.

Anto Rogan is a tall, overweight, sixteen-year-old with ginger hair and an attempted moustache. He is wearing a brand-new Celtic football shirt with several unfortunate paint stains and a pair of grey tracksuit bottoms from the bargain bucket in George at Asda. He has an unlit cigarette behind one ear and a single gold stud earring in the other.

'Watch out,' he calls to anyone in earshot, 'here come the Orange Teletubbies!'

The words halt Roberta and Jean in their tracks but Roberta is having none of this.

'You watch your lip, wee lad,' she responds in an act of defiance, 'or I'll give you a good slap on the bake!'

Seamie turns around and looks at the two women sternly, as if they have broken an obvious rule. He sniffs deliberately before enquiring, 'What are yousens doin' on our side anyway?'

Seamie McGuigan is a wiry seventeen-year-old wearing a faded designer tracksuit and a Burberry baseball cap. Jean notices that his dark hair is as closely shaved as Sam's the previous week, except his millimetre fringe is gelled upwards into a spike. She also notices the poorly inked IRA tattoo on his inner forearm, the scars on his wrist and his very sad eyes.

'You listen to me, son,' replies Jean, 'we're goin' round to the wee pensioners' club in our church. That church was here on this road long before you were even a twinkle in your mammy's eye.'

'Well, your sort don't live on this side any more,' retorts Seamie, 'so why don't youse just clear off and take your Orange church with ye?' Seamie sniffs aggressively, wipes his nose and turns away in disgust, as if he wishes to waste no more time with these people.

He returns to painting the graffiti with added enthusiasm. When he turns away Jean notices a long scar on his neck from his chin to the neckline of his shirt. She winces at the sight of this injury.

However, Anto decides he is not finished with these two oul dolls. 'Aye! Aye! Yer ma!' he shouts and stares and cocks his head with an aggressive tick.

Despite appearances Anto comes from a happy family home. An only child, his parents have spoiled him, but he sometimes tells his mates that his father beats him with a belt for taking drugs – even though the only drugs he takes are paracetamol for a cold. If Seamie and his mates knew that Anto's mammy still makes him a hot chocolate with marshmallows and a hot-water bottle every night, his life would not be worth living.

'Well, what are you lookin' at, oul doll?' he sneers.

'I'd love to give that wee hallion a good dig in the gub, so I would!' says Roberta. She takes two steps closer to the antagonistic teenager. 'Don't you dare talk to Wee Jean like that!' she shouts through the transparency of her umbrella. 'Her grandson's fighting Obama Bin Aladdin's mates in Iraq.'

'Wha?' replies Anto.

Jean shakes her head.

Seamie continues to paint while addressing the women behind him. 'Well, my granda fought the fuckin' Brits right here on this street!' he announces.

'Aye!' says Anto, 'and your side shot him in the head when he got outta Long Kesh!'

Seamie turns around and glares at Anto for sharing such painful and private information with the enemy. Anto notices his offence immediately and is downcast to have upset Seamie.

'Wee lad, I never shot nobody in my life,' says Jean.

She takes a closer look at Seamie and tries to establish eye contact. She notices his sad eyes are dark blue and she decides he is a good-looking lad even with his shaven head and pale, gaunt face. She thinks for a moment and then continues with carefully chosen words.

'I'm very sorry about your granda, son,' she says, 'but it sounds like he might've been doin' a wee bit of shootin' himself.'

'And what would you know, missus?' snaps Seamie.

Anto barges in front of Seamie to protect him from this assault on his grandfather's honour. Anto tries to copy Seamie with the same small stud earring in one ear, although his clothes are cheaper versions of his hero's attire. He wants so much to be like Seamie but his own grandfather was not a republican hero. His granda was a porter in the Royal Victoria Hospital during the Troubles and he spent most of his spare time going to prayer meetings for peace in Clonard Monastery.

'Seamie's granda fought for freedom for Ireland from the Brits,' he proclaims, 'and I'll fight the Brits too, to get youse out of Ireland once and for all, so I will!'

'Wind yer neck in, wee lad,' says Jean. 'Your head's cut, so it is!'

Anto is unaware that Seamie is rolling his eyes at this act of bravado. Meanwhile Roberta grabs hold of Jean's arm.

'Oh, my God, Jean, these two are diffident republicans – come on, quick!'

Seamie laughs and Anto scowls at the reaction of these two annoying wee Protestant women. Roberta tries to pull Jean away from the two teenagers but Jean resists and stands her ground.

'Houl your horses, Roberta,' she tells her friend and turns back towards the two young men. 'Son, we go round here every Wednesday mornin' and meet with weemin from your side,' she attempts to explain.

'They're traitors then!' barks Anto.

Seamie's back is turned but his shoulders rise and fall indicating stifled laughter.

Roberta is affronted by this attack on her Catholic friends. 'Well, Wee Patricia goes to the cross-community pensioners' club every single week, and them there loyalist paramilitaries blew her legs off at the post office, so they did!' she asserts.

'Is that yer mental woman in the wheelchair with the wee Protestant dog?' checks Anto.

'She's a space cadet!' interjects Seamie.

'Don't you dare talk about our good friends Patricia and Bridget like that, wee lad!' says Jean.

'Aye,' says Roberta, 'Wee Jean made Bridget a lovely pavlova for the wake when her Gerard died.'

'And Bridget's father was in the old IRA, ya know,' adds Jean.

'Wha?' says Anto.

'So what, missus?' says Seamie pointing in the direction of the church steeple, 'youse are all wastin' your time in there anyway.'

The women step back quickly to avoid splashes of paint flying from his brush.

'There's no one up there listenin',' says Seamie, now pointing his paintbrush heavenward.

Roberta cannot cope with this. She shakes her head and covers her ears at such blasphemy.

'Don't go slabberin' like that to me, son,' responds Jean. 'Just because I go to church and all doesn't mean I'm some wee good-livin' granny, ye know. I'll take my fist to you if there's any more of yer oul lip!'

Seamie can no longer contain his laughter. 'Aye!' he says.

'Aye, right, dead on!'

Anto joins in with his best attempt at a mocking jeer, 'Aye, yer MA!'

Jean is more concerned with trying to reason with the two young men. She remembers the worst-behaved children in the dinner hall always needed just a wee bit of extra attention and you could talk some sense into them, especially if you got them on their own for a minute or two. She understood that if you got the troublemaker away from their peers and had a quiet word, you could make more progress than shouting at them a dozen times over coagulating pink custard.

'Why can't youse make friends with the wee lads over on our side instead of keepin' all this friggin' fightin' goin'?' she says, accentuating every word with a jolt of her umbrella. 'Youse are all just the same, you know.'

'And what would oul dolls like youse two know about it?' Seamie answers with a further sniff, turning his back on the two women once more.

'C'mon, Anto!' he calls to his sidekick, as if the women have disappeared forever.

Anto smiles at this call of approval.

Seamie finishes the final letter of the sectarian slogan and hurls the remainder of the paint tin over the gate, just like Sam the week before. Only his insult is different. 'Orange bastards!' he yells triumphantly and looks back at Jean and Roberta with a defiant look that clearly says – and that means you two oul dolls too!

With renewed enthusiasm now, Anto lifts a red brick and attempts to hurl it across the peace gate, but he is not spatially aware and the projectile misfires and the brick falls back down towards him as he shouts, '*Tiochfaidh ár—*'

The brick hits his head.

'Fuck!'

Seamie creases over with laughter.

Anto holds his injured head.

'What are you gonna tell your ma?' says Seamie laughing.

'I'll say them Prods done a vicious sectarian attack on my head across the peace wall!'

'Will you tell her it was two oul dolls?' mocks Seamie.

'Wise up, Seamie!' says Anto and walks off towards home in the huffs.

Jean and Roberta hurry away towards the open door of the church looking more determined than scared.

'Them wee lads are a nightmare!' says Roberta.

'C'mon, Roberta,' says Jean. 'My Derek always said don't get involved, but I'm tellin' you this, and I'm tellin' it till you now, and I'm tellin' it till you for nathin' – I've had enough! That's decided it for me. I'm goin' to *do* somethin' about this bloody place!'

6

Undeterred by the latest intergenerational spat, Roberta and
Jean arrive at the cross-community pensioners' club in one of
the small, draughty meeting rooms in the faded Methodist
church hall.

'Sit down, Roberta, them wee lads would take the legs from
under ye,' says Jean.

'Tell me about it!' says Patricia.

Sixty years ago this church attracted a thriving congregation
of families from the surrounding streets. Dressed in their
Sunday best, fathers cleaned up from the foundry, mothers
fresh from the mill and children attending the Sunday school
gathered here faithfully every week. Today the church is a sad
remnant of a more religious past. These days the once
flourishing church is frequented by a handful of surviving
senior citizens clinging to the past, along with an interesting
collection of social misfits who no one else gives the time of
day to but who have found some acceptance and belonging
here. When you have barely thirty parishioners remaining, a
church finally loses the luxury of excluding the people society
shuns the most.

A small wooden table fills the centre of the meeting room
and this is surrounded by wooden foldable chairs carved with
innocent graffiti from the 1950s: *Billy loves Margaret* and
Linfield FC are smoothed into the grain. Most of the church's
chairs are in storage now due to the dramatic decrease in
demand for worshipful sitting. There is a slightly faded colour
poster on the wall of a handshake and a rainbow that says
Love Your Neighbour. Various other posters advertise a range

of community events including a car boot sale for church-roof repairs, a karaoke night for Cancer Research and a mother-and-toddler group. These are the signs the latest minister is working against the odds to make his declining church relevant.

Someone has forgotten to remove last year's poster for the cross-community Santa's grotto, perhaps because it had been regarded by the whole community as a great success. Not one person had asked whether Father Christmas was a Protestant or a Catholic, and several people had compared the grotto to the Belfast Co-op's in the 1960s before the IRA had blown it up – high praise indeed (being compared to the Co-op, that is, not the Co-op being selected for destruction by the IRA).

This is what the women love about this place. It reminds them of working together in the stitching factories before the Troubles, before the riots and barricades, before the bombs and the soldiers, when everyone knew what religion you were but still worked and joked and socialised with you anyway.

Bridget is busily pouring tea into plain white cups nestled on saucers. The previous formality of this religious institution is long gone, but this is a place where the respectability of a china cup and saucer survives. A nice cup of tea can calm many nerves and break down all sorts of barriers in Belfast.

By now Jean and Roberta have shaken off both the rain and the verbal abuse from outside this little sanctuary and are proudly presenting the precious box of tray bakes. Patricia is poised at the top of the table with Wee Jack Surgeoner now permanently planted in her lap and panting excitedly at the gathering of people.

'Well, Bridget,' says Jean, 'what are we going to do about this gate? Tea, Roberta?'

'Big Isobel's funeral was the last straw for me,' answers Bridget. 'Tea, Patricia?'

'Yes, love,' says Patricia, as Wee Jack licks her cheek. 'Last night I told my Liam if I still had my legs, I'd run straight out there and start pullin' it down with my bare hands!'

Bridget has known Patricia since the day she was born. In fact, Bridget delivered Patricia in the Royal Victoria Hospital, just down the road from here. Bridget delivered a sizeable proportion of the residents of West Belfast regardless of religion.

'We all arrive into this world the same,' she would often say in response to the latest news of intolerance in her city or in distant lands, 'and we all leave the same way too. So there's no need for all the unkindness and cruelty in between.'

Bridget has deep admiration for Patricia's understated courage. She visited Patricia in the Royal every day after the bomb, when it looked as if Patricia might not survive her injuries. Even on days when poor Liam couldn't face the horror of it all, Bridget would pop over to Patricia's ward, between births, and hold her hand and say a prayer with her rosary beads until the day when her young friend eventually came home in a wheelchair. Then Bridget visited Patricia on her afternoons off and on the days when Liam was at the bookies or away fishing.

Bridget was there in the very darkest of days when Patricia didn't think she could go on living. Only Bridget knows that Patricia believed God was punishing her for the secret sin of giving up her baby boy for adoption when she was fifteen, before she met Liam. Later still Bridget had privately helped Patricia accept that her only daughter being unable to have children of her own was not yet further punishment from an angry God. 'Well, do you not think you've been punished enough yourself by now?' Bridget would say.

These words helped a great deal because Patricia accepted Bridget's superior knowledge on all things both theological and gynaecological. Bridget still remembers the day Patricia told her, 'Well, Bridget, I've two choices. Give up or get on with it. And I'm bloody sure I'm not givin' up over the head of them dickheads that planted that bomb at the post office!'

Bridget admired Patricia's determination to get on with her life. She respected her choice to waste no more time and energy on bitterness and hatred towards the men who had mutilated her for their cause. Bridget was unsure she could be so forgiving herself if she had been disabled in such a cruel manner. But despite this, she is well aware of how impulsive and impractical Patricia can be at times, and today is a good example of this.

'It's not as simple as going outside and taking the wall down with your own bare hands, Patricia,' she points out. 'A lot of people are scared of the peace gate opening, so they are. They feel safer with the walls. They think it protects them. Tea, Jean?'

'Yes, just half full, Bridget, love,' says Jean. 'Them wee lads don't remember what it was like round here before them walls went up. Sure, we lived in the same streets round here and there were some Prods on the Falls and some Catholics on the Shankill and no one never even bothered.'

Bridget points at her head. 'It's the walls in here that need to come down first,' she says.

All the women nod at Bridget's wisdom. At eighty-nine she is the oldest and wisest retired midwife in West Belfast. Bridget's mother died at the age of ninety-nine and so the women regularly predict, 'Our Bridget'll see a hundred, so she will.'

Jean and Roberta sit down at the table as Bridget pours yet more tea and the tray bake supply gradually diminishes. Once she has settled herself, Jean decides it's time to speak up and she takes a deep breath.

'Right, girls, my Derek always told me to keep your head down if you want a quiet life in this country,' she begins quietly.

'Aye, my Liam's the same – "Whatever ya say, say nathin and you'll have no trouble",' adds Patricia.

'But where has keepin' my head down got me?' asks Jean. 'My own family don't want to live here no more even though there's peace nigh.'

It was during moments like this that Jean recalled all that had happened to Derek. She still missed her dear husband every single day. She could never forget the threats and intimidation he received for working for Catholics and then again for doing work in a police station. Derek was the victim of true cross-community intimidation for daring to take any offer of work regardless of sectarian sensibilities. As far as Jean is concerned he will always be her wee bricklayer with the brown eyes from Berlin Street. How ironic that her much-missed husband spent his entire life building walls regardless of the community and now Jean wants to tear down the walls that separate the same community.

Jean's announcement indicates that the meeting has commenced and Bridget sits down at the table with the other women to consider the serious business of the day.

'Oh, I know,' says Bridget with a slight wince as her arthritic hip catches in the seated position, 'all my boys across the water are the same. No intention of coming back here. "Mammy, you know we love you and Belfast is our home, but we're thinking of the children," they say. So much for our so-called peace dividend.'

'Is that like when you used to get your Co-op dividend down in York Street?' asks Roberta.

Jean resists the temptation to attempt an explanation.

'My Bernadette didn't leave Ireland,' says Patricia. 'She married a wee Scotch fella and he's a Protestant teacher in Magherafelt and they never come next nor near West Belfast neither.'

'Well, at least my Niamh still visits me,' Bridget interjects with a slight haughtiness.

'Sure, your Niamh married that wee foreign doctor and moved to South Africa' says Patricia. 'You only see them every of couple years.'

'Aye, right nuff, Bridget,' says Roberta, 'he was a lovely wee Indian fella like from one of them Ballywood movies.'

'Aye, but he got fed up here bein' asked whether he was a Catholic Muslim or a Protestant Muslim,' says Patricia.

Bridget casts disapproving stares around the room. Bridget likes her privacy and this is sensitive territory. An air of tension rises between the old friends. After a few moments of silence, broken only by the slight tinkle of shaking cups and saucers in elderly hands, everyone knows it's time to change the subject.

'Well, I'll tell ya what, girls, and I'll tell you the truth, and I'll tell it to youse for nathin',' says Jean, 'I've kept my head down long enough in this bloody place. Are we gonna be livin' behind these gates and walls forever?'

'Aye, they knocked down that big wall in Berlin ages ago. Kylie was still in *Neighbours*, so she was,' says Roberta, 'and now that oul rip Trump is buildin' another big wall to keep all the Mexican terrorists from doin' another 5/11 in America!'

'And, sure, there's been no trouble at half the gates for ages anyway,' adds Patricia, 'and the only reason the childer come to the wall to throw stones is because there's a wall to try to get your stone over!'

'It causes the trouble instead of stopping it,' says Bridget.

She looks around the table at her friends. Bridget knows these women so well. She knows all their ups and downs, their joys and sorrows. She has listened to the stories of money troubles, lost babies, bereavements and health scares. In this very room the women completed a host of adult education courses on everything from flower arranging to human rights. Bridget has sat around this table with this same group of women to discuss traffic calming, schools closing, parades, riots, antisocial behaviour and dog poo. It would be a brave or foolish man who tried to patronise this group of women, she thinks. Bridget knows just how tough and determined the women of West Belfast can be.

'I think we should start a campaign,' Bridget announces. 'A wee campaign to get the gate opened – at least during the day, before the wee hoods get out of bed and come out for a riot.'

'Brilliant, Bridget!' exclaims Jean enthusiastically. 'Where would we be without your brains, love?'

'Oh, our Bridget's no dozer!' smiles Roberta.

'I'm up for that,' affirms Patricia, her large brown eyes widening at the wonder of the idea. 'C'mon nigh, girls, we'll call the campaign – Get Our Gate Open.'

'That's the G-O-G-O Campaign. The GOGO Campaign!' laughs Bridget.

'Oh, here! That means we're the … the GOGO Girls!' exclaims Jean.

The women laugh together for a while before becoming suddenly quiet and thoughtful. It feels as if they are being called together on an adventure for the sake of a better future.

'I'm scared,' says Roberta soberly. 'You know what some of themuns are like round here. And there's still the paramilitaries and all.'

'Oh, I know all about them, love,' says Bridget. 'I delivered most of them in the Royal.' She pauses, looks at each of her friends intently and adds, 'If we do this, girls, you have to remember, there will be no turning back. Our old lives will be over, I promise you.'

'I'll go straight out there myself, right now, and start a protest, and I'll ring Stephen Nolan on the BBC and we'll see if anyone tries till stop me!' exclaims Patricia indignantly.

But Roberta is having doubts. 'What difference could a group of oul dolls like us make?' she asks. 'What do you think, Jean?'

Jean pauses for a moment before standing up slowly. She straightens her aching back and speaks. 'Bridget's right,' she begins, 'there'll be no turnin' back. But are we just gonna sit here and drink cups of tea like wee old ladies for the rest of our lives?'

'Oh, Jean!' cries Roberta, 'are you sayin' we should follow our dreams … like … like Susan Boyle?'

Patricia bangs her fist on the table and shouts, 'Well, I wanna be a GOGO Girl!'

Wee Jack stands up in Patricia's lap and his tail wags around in circles as fast as a helicopter blade.

Bridget stands up and announces, 'And I'm going to be a GOGO Girl!'

Roberta stands up and follows with her declaration, 'When I was young, I always wanted to be a GOGO Girl.'

For a second the women look at Roberta in confusion.

'So we are the GOGO Girls,' proclaims Jean, 'and we are not keepin' our heads down no more!'

'It's girl power – we're like the Spice Girls but with bad hips!' says Patricia.

The women applaud as Jean continues, 'We're goin' to get that gate opened every day. We are goin' to make this road a safer place – a better place for all of us.'

Wee Jack is barking enthusiastically now.

Roberta cannot contain her admiration. 'Oh, Jean,' she says, 'you'll be our leader, won't you? You're like yer woman Angela Miracle in Germany!'

'All together girls – Get Our Gate Open!' leads Patricia with a rhythmic thump of protest on the wooden table.

The women begin to bang the table with teaspoons and in unison they chant together:

'Get Our Gate Open!'

'Get Our Gate Open!'

'Get Our Gate Open!'

The banging on the table shakes loose crumbs from the tray bakes onto the saucers, and the teacups seem to shiver in the midst of the resolute vibrations. Wee Jack Surgeoner continues to bark the most approving of barks, as if Big Isobel herself is agreeing from beyond the grave.

Outside, a magpie settles on the church steeple, attracted by the ominous squawks coming from inside the building below. The magpie's head twitches from side to side. The bird releases a flow of pure white shit that trickles down the sides of the spire.

7

In Belfast city centre shoppers are carrying designer handbags up and down the grand escalators at the heart of the impressive Victoria Square Shopping Centre. In the Titanic Quarter, alongside the flourishing film studios and technology hubs, tourists from all over the world are queuing to get into the *Titanic* museum. Scores of new hotels in the city centre are hosting prestigious conferences and outrageous stag parties and bars and restaurants are thriving day and night. But just one mile away, up the road, the GOGO Girls are struggling with the thirty-foot-high legacy of a past that no one else in this modern, vibrant city seems to care about. This barrier has outlived the Berlin Wall and divided Belfast for longer. At the very end of the twentieth century the city of Belfast began to rise from the ashes of thirty years of conflict. The huge British army installations are long gone and the security barriers that once circled the city centre are a distant memory, but the many miles of peace walls separating the poorest Catholic and Protestant neighbourhoods remain.

'You have the heart of a lion, Jean,' says Patricia.

'I'm just tryin' to do the right thing,' says Jean.

Today the GOGO Campaign is moving up a level. Jean and Patricia are perched excitedly at Jean's spotless kitchen table, complete with two cups of tea, of course, and a plentiful pavlova. Patricia is holding the telephone to one ear and has her forefinger in the other ear as Wee Jack hoovers up pavlova particles from her lap.

'Are you never on yet?' whispers Jean. 'Oh, my nerves are bad! They'll never let the likes of us on the radio, so they'll not.'

'Shush, you!' replies Patricia. 'He says they mightn't have time to put me on the day cause one of them oul MLAs has been up to somethin' ratten again.'

Every few minutes Patricia overhears a disembodied voice on the other end of the phone, 'It's yer man again … Is there no one else?' and then she hears Stephen himself saying, 'Every phone line into the station is jammed this morning!' Her hopes rise and fall as she tries to translate these faint communications into some indication of whether her time has finally come.

Patricia dreamt of appearing on *The Nolan Show* on BBC Radio Ulster ever since she had listened to the episodes about Northern Ireland's politicians burning millions of pounds of wood pellets to save the environment. Patricia loved listening to everyone being angry at the politicians they kept re-electing, and she adored the presenter whom she always defended against his critics, saying he was 'a lovely big fella with his mammy and his weight and all'. She never missed the morning radio phone-in and although she had called into the programme many times, she had never managed to get her voice on the airwaves.

Patricia had attempted to share her anger with the whole of Northern Ireland when politicians were being nasty to the other side about parades and when everyone was fighting over gay cakes, but she worried she had never been outraged enough. She had the urge to share her grief with the world when Frank Carson and Vera Duckworth died but she could never get through on the busy phone lines in time to talk to her beloved presenter. On one occasion a middle-class voice on the other end of the phone had agreed to allow her on the radio to complain about dogs' dirt on the beach in Bangor. She waited on the phone for almost an hour until her battery was nearly empty, but she was dropped at the last minute because a paramilitary leader wouldn't stop talking about all the injustices against 'his community', and then an MP phoned up to be angry about something in the 1970s.

Surely today it will be different. This morning it will be Patricia's turn. Jean takes a small compact from her apron pocket and begins to apply her traditional foundation and light blusher. Although she knows this is radio and Patricia will be doing all the talking, Jean still feels she wants to look her best for the occasion of the GOGO Girls' first media appearance.

'Och, you were lovely in your day, Jean,' compliments Patricia.

Jean responds with a half-smile, but before Patricia can work out that her remark was not received entirely as flattering, she hears the much-adored and longed-for voice on the other end of the phone. Patricia sits up rigidly as if an electrical current has passed through her body. Wee Jack sits up too and his terrier ears twitch.

'Hello? Hello ... Stephen, is that you?' says Patricia, waving her hand at Jean before pointing to the phone, her eyes wide open with excitement.

Jean nods enthusiastically. Wee Jack wags his tail. Patricia can hardly believe her dream has finally come true.

'Yes, er ... Stephen, love,' begins Patricia, taking a deep breath and continuing, 'it's Patricia here from the West Belfast GOGO Girls ... what, love? Aye, Stephen, it stands for Get Our Gate Open ...'

Jean nods encouragingly. Wee Jack pants. Thousands of people across Northern Ireland are listening to every word, waiting to be outraged or offended.

'Well, Stephen, love, we're startin' a campaign to get the peace gate open, so we're phonin' you to help us, on the biggest show in the country ... We're the GOGO Girls and we want the peace gate opened because Big Isobel got stuck in it in her coffin and it's a blinkin' disgrace ... And we want to go and see our wee friends on the other side whenever we want and we don't need it any more, so we don't, and, sure, we've had peace for twenty years now, and we're sick of all that oul nonsense, and instead of themuns at Stormount wasting billions of pounds burnin' all them wooden parrots down in Fermanagh, like you told us, Stephen, they should be usin' the money to take these gates away as long as they put up speed ramps on the road because we've got used to no traffic in our street, right nuff, and we're worried about the wee childer ... And I think you're a lovely big fella with your mammy and your diet and all ...'

Poor Stephen Nolan, even with his mastery of interrupting lying politicians, barely gets a word in edgeways.

'Let me tell you all about the GOGO Girls, Stephen,' she continues, and introduces the world to the campaign.

'Thank you, Patricia, we really do need to go to the news now. It's three minutes late already,' says the BBC presenter after a further five-minute monologue.

The GOGO Girls stay tuned as listeners from all over Northern Ireland phone in to give their reactions to the campaign. Two women from either side of the peace wall in East Belfast support the GOGO Campaign and say it's a great idea, so it is, and they would love the walls to come down on their side of town. The leader of a residents' group in North Belfast calls to complain that the women hadn't consulted him before starting the campaign and says they had better not interfere with any of his walls. A community worker from an estate in Bangor, a place with no peace walls at all, phones in to say it is up to residents who live beside the peace walls to decide whether they come down or not and not middle-class do-gooders from the leafy suburbs like Patricia. A man from Ballymoney stays on the line and keeps interrupting everybody to explain that if everyone listening simply accepted the Lord Jesus Christ as their own personal Saviour then all the gates would be opened overnight. A councillor from Ballymena is asked if he would support the women's group and he says as long as they aren't lesbians he wouldn't stand in their way.

Finally, a taxi driver from Newry suggests that the only way to stop violence at the peace wall is 'to round up all the wee scumbegs and have the wee bastards birched in public'. Stephen fades him out just before he explains which of the various body parts of the wee scumbegs he would cut off first. Stephen Nolan himself is very encouraging and only calls Patricia an 'oul doll' once, when she gets distracted from the campaign and starts flirting with him to come up to West Belfast and give her a wee push in her wheelchair.

Wee Jack just barks twice and Jean has to put him outside in the hall where he chews up a Methodist hymn book and a leaflet on making a will from the Citizens' Advice Bureau.

Bridget and Roberta arrive and having analysed every second of the radio show, the GOGO Girls conclude that this media exposure has been a great success for the launch of the campaign. The women's phones do not stop ringing for the next few hours. Most people are very encouraging, although several friends tell the women they need to 'watch themselves for speaking up'. Only two anonymous callers tell them to fuck off and mind their own business. In contrast, dozens of neighbours and journalists and PhD students demand more information about the GOGO Girls and their plans for opening a peace gate in West Belfast. Patricia is jubilant.

'We're like *The Real Housewives* of West Belfast!' cries Patricia.

'What's that?' asks Bridget.

'It's one of them reality TV programmes that Roberta watches all the time, Bridget,' explains Jean.

'Yes, Bridget, love, but it's a wee bit more like *Keeping Up with the Kardashians* than I'm a Celibate … Get Me Out of This Here Jungle!,' adds Roberta.

Bridget looks at Roberta as if she is speaking another language.

'Well, I think I'll stick to *Antiques Roadshow*. That's enough reality for me, thank you very much,' says Bridget.

Of course, the reality for the women is that now their campaign has gone public there will be no turning back. Although no one says it out loud, the women sense that today they crossed a threshold into the unknown, and they are old enough and wise enough to realise that by moving beyond their boundaries in Belfast there may be trouble ahead.

8

A massive 'Get Our Gate Open' banner is now draped along the wall of the cross-community pensioners' club meeting room. Patricia's Liam donated the funds for the banner from a win on the horses on the day of her Nolan interview. The banner obscures nearly all the other posters and notices, apart from the one advertising last year's legendary cross-community Santa's grotto, of course. It's only a few weeks since Big Isobel's funeral but today the women have a sense of momentum and some supportive public opinion behind them.

'We can do this, girls,' Jean reminds the team.

'*Yes We Can!*' says Roberta. 'Like what Osama said!'

'My Liam says everyone in the bookies thought I was great on Nolan,' boasts Patricia.

'A wee man walkin' his fox terrier stopped me in Woodvale Park and handed me a fiver to go towards the campaign,' says Roberta.

'I got a phone call from my cousins in Dublin,' says Bridget. 'They've even heard about us in the south, and as you know they're generally not a bit interested in the north down there.'

This is all that matters now. The women are committed to meeting together every week to plan the campaign. All the most important people in their community, from both sides, are invited along to hear about the plans. The women are determined to gain their support. In one of their adult education courses the group had learned about lobbying stakeholders, and once Roberta was reassured that stakeholders were not scary people who wanted to kill vampires they had learned a great deal. The women now have a list of the most influential people in their community and they are inviting them for a cup of tea and a chat about how to get the peace gate opened. This is the first such meeting with one of these special guests and so the women are naturally a little nervous.

'Oh, I think he's here!' says Patricia apprehensively, fixing her hair.

'Well, here goes nathin',' says Jean and takes a deep breath.

A large man with significant muscles, loyalist tattoos and chunky gold jewellery enters the room. A certain unspoken authority arrives with him. He sits down awkwardly on an office swivel chair (borrowed from the minister) at the top of the table.

'Tea, love?' asks Jean.

'Aye, dead on,' replies the guest.

The man is poured a nice cup of tea by Bridget. He is accustomed to service and attention. This is Big Stan, the chairman of the Loyalist Interface Group, also known as LIG for short. His driver is waiting outside having a smoke. Big Stan is much feared and hated by the local teenagers, such as Sam and Lee, who steal Ford Fiestas for the craic, but this 'community leader' is neither feared or hated by Jean who remembers when young Stanley was himself a teenager stealing Vauxhall Vivas to block the roads for Ulster. Jean remembers how young Stanley's mother used to worry that he was still wetting the bed when he was ten years old. Jean always felt sorry for young Stanley and gave him extra pink custard on his jam sponge at school, even though the other dinner ladies disapproved of her having 'wee favourites'.

Jean recalls Stanley's mother's joy when he was released from jail at the end of the Troubles. 'Stanley's a good boy, so he is, Jean,' she said. 'He just got in with a bad crowd,' she said. Aye, and became their brigadier! Jean thought, but kept these words to herself.

Jean is glad to see Stanley's transformation from paramilitary leader to community worker. She thinks he genuinely wants the best for the community, but she doesn't like the way he barks orders at the youngsters and gives the impression he is still in charge of the whole street. Big Stan decides for himself when the paramilitary flags go up on the lampposts and if and when they come down. On this matter he is beyond question and no one dares challenge him – not the church or the politicians or the police. Big Stan is a very powerful man in these parts and he knows it. He attends community meetings with Belfast City Council and accuses all the government agencies of neglecting and damaging his community. Not one of these statutory bodies dares speak up to suggest that Big Stan and his paramilitary minions may also be damaging his community.

As the meeting begins, Roberta offers Big Stan a large, heavily buttered cherry scone. Big Stan is disarmed by the oversized cake and it's a long time since anyone has disarmed Big Stan.

'My community do nat want no gates opened,' he announces. 'Nat until the other side stops their unprovoked sectarian attacks on my culture!'

Unfortunately the swivel chair on which Big Stan is seated is not robust enough to carry his considerable weight, and so at just the wrong moment the chair begins to lower, leaving Big Stan looking uncharacteristically small as if shrinking beneath the table. The chair sinks down slowly and Big Stan's knees are now at the height of his chest.

Wee Jack Surgeoner opens an eye and stares at Big Stan from Patricia's lap and Roberta stifles a chuckle.

'Do you take sugar, love?' panics Bridget.

'Do you wanna wee fruit scone in your hand for your driver, Big Stan?' offers Roberta.

Jean interrupts, 'Well, I've lived in *your* community since before you were born, love, and I live right here beside the gate, and I want it open, so I do.'

Roberta and Patricia swallow loudly in unison. Wee Jack gazes up at Patricia and lets out a tiny whine. Big Stan looks at Jean in disbelief. He is clearly unaccustomed to contradiction and the look of surprise remains on his face as he shakes his head, gets up and excuses himself to go to another, more important, meeting about bonfires. The encounter lasted no more than three minutes. Big Stan barely sipped his tea and took only one mouthful of scone. By any measurement this could not be regarded as a successful start to lobbying stakeholders.

'I thought he was goin' to wet himself!' says Patricia.

Jean controls her urge to make further obvious comment.

'Nightmare!' says Roberta.

'Jean, love, I think we're wasting our time with him,' says Bridget. 'Sure, do you remember the time he held a protest outside your wee primary school because he said they were teaching the children to sing in Irish for the school concert.'

'Oh, don't remind me!' says Jean. 'The children weren't even singin' a word in Irish. The big eejit had called in to collect his grandson and he overheard the wee choir practising "Hakuna Matata" from *The Lion King*!'

The following week the VIP guest is Wee Malachy from the Republican Interface Group, also known as RIG. Wee Malachy is small and thin with closely cropped grey hair, wearing a leather bomber jacket, light blue jeans and a Che Guevara T-shirt.

Roberta offers Wee Malachy an apple puff pastry bulging with fresh cream.

'Tea, love?' asks Bridget.

'Just a wee drop,' replies Wee Malachy.

When Bridget pours his tea her hands are shaking slightly more noticeably than usual. Bridget delivered Wee Malachy in the Royal fifty-nine years ago, and forty years ago he hijacked her car to blow up the wee sweetie shop. She knows he works twenty-four hours a day for the community now, but she still remembers him threatening to blow her fucking head off if she didn't give up her beloved Austin Allegro to bomb a confectionery provider in the struggle for Irish freedom. It's an incident Wee Malachy has clearly forgotten as a minor detail in the struggle against the British war machine, but Bridget will never forget.

The women have ensured the screws under the seat of the swivel chair have been tightened to avoid another embarrassing incident with a community leader.

'Let me be very clear, my community do nat want no gates opened,' begins Wee Malachy, struggling with fresh cream leaking onto his greying goatee beard. 'Nat until we have guarantees we will be treated with respect and complete equality by the people on the other side of the wall.'

'Sure, we'll open the gate in Irish too, love, if you want,' assures Roberta.

A dollop of fresh cream drips disrespectfully onto Wee Malachy's boots. Patricia drops her teaspoon. Wee Jack leaps out of her lap and edges slowly towards Wee Malachy until he can lick his boots and traces of fresh cream discreetly.

'Are you sure you don't want a wee box of tray bakes for all your staff at the community centre, love?' asks Jean.

Bridget interrupts with uncharacteristic curtness, 'Wait till I tell you, son.' She points at Jean and Roberta. 'These women have *equally* as big a problem making ends meet with their pension as I do.'

Roberta chokes on her milky tea.

Wee Malachy is clearly affronted by Bridget's impertinence. He is used to being the outraged victim of authority and struggles not to say that this cheeky oul doll should stick to looking after wee babies and minding her own fucking business, because he knows you aren't allowed to say that sort of thing out loud any more.

Patricia fiddles nervously with the controls of her electric wheelchair and accidently jolts forwards causing Wee Malachy to spill more cream from his apple puff pastry down the front of his T-shirt, all over Che Guevara's beret. As Wee Malachy excuses himself to go to a more important meeting about parades' protests, Jean notices that it looks as if a seagull has shit on Che. When the door closes behind him, Patricia can no longer contain herself.

'Oh, that wee gabshite has the sort of face on him I'd never get tired kickin' – if I had my legs!'

'If that's a stakeholder, he can keep his oul stakes,' Roberta announces.

Bridget and Jean quietly pray that Wee Malachy is out of earshot.

The next week the visiting VIP is a Presbyterian minister, a sober, obese man with a red face, greasy skin and particularly plump fingers. Just before he arrives, Roberta expresses her reservations.

'I know he's a clergyman and all, and we need him to bury us one day, but I stopped goin' to the jumble sales in his church after they voted to stop christenin' the wee gay babies. I heard he won't even do the wee hero-sexual babies if the parents aren't good-livin' too.'

'I know he hasn't a baldy notion,' says Jean, 'but at least he wants to talk to us. That oul Free Presbyterian down the road said he wouldn't even come to our wee meetin' because he says it's joint worship with Rome.'

'I'd join my boot with his arse if I had one,' says Patricia at just the wrong moment, as the minister enters the room.

The portly clergyman fills his plate with a substantial selection of pastries and consumes all with avarice while Bridget replenishes his teacup. Roberta stares a little too intently in fascination at how his pink double chin spills over his dog collar, and offers the reverend a further familiar smorgasbord of tray bakes as Jean begins the meeting.

'Oh, it sounds like a wonderful idea, ladies,' he proclaims, looking at his empty teacup and awaiting a refill. 'More tea, please, ladies?'

This is a man who is accustomed to women pouring him tea. Jean pours him a second cup somewhat resentfully. She has attended church every week of her life but never fails to be disappointed by religious people, especially men who regard her only contribution to the life of the church as tea-pouring and sandwich-making duties. Jean recalls hearing a visiting minister from South Africa preaching that the church should help the poor and be involved in breaking down barriers of hatred between different people. She remembers wondering why there were not more missionaries from Africa coming to preach this message in the churches of Northern Ireland.

'Of course, it's important for us, as Presbyterians, to first study God's Word to discern if there is indeed a biblical mandate for Christian people to engage in such activities,' explains the portly clergyman. 'The question must be asked – is there indeed a theological imperative for opening the peace gate?'

Jean points to the partly obscured poster on the wall. 'You mean like *Love Your Neighbour*?'

The minister looks shocked at Jean's intervention. Decades of preaching in his pulpit at six feet above contradiction make such challenges from uneducated parishioners deeply uncomfortable. Suddenly Wee Jack jumps into his lap and begins sniffing his crotch region inappropriately.

'Well, I must say you ladies really have excelled yourselves with the refreshments this morning,' he says, wincing slightly and brushing the dog from his lap. He makes swift excuses and departs to a more important meeting about a dispute over the church flower rota.

As the door slams in his wake Roberta says, 'I know he's one of ours, so he is, Jean, but that man's more borin' than bloody Brexit!'

Finally, to complete this first set of weekly meetings, and to maintain the necessary religious balance, the next special guest is a tall, thin Catholic priest with small round glasses and no hair whatsoever. Patricia had assured the other women he is one of the good priests because he put a cap on financial gifts at First Holy Communion. Patricia is not easily impressed by the clergy. At the parish bingo, in front of everyone, she had accused the previous parish priest of being 'more against integrated schools than against bloody child abusers!'.

However, Bridget is a more traditional Catholic and feels a modicum of respect is required to acknowledge the visit of a parish priest. She remembers the days when you bowed and kissed the ring of a bishop, and when the absolution of a priest in the confession box was the forgiveness of God. Over the years she has despaired at revelations of child abuse and cover-ups. Her love for the Church simply exacerbated her pain at the wickedness exposed within. For years her ecumenical outlook has been out of sync with some in her parish who quietly disapprove of her praying with heretical Protestants, and in recent years Bridget entertained more rebellious thoughts about the possibility of married priests and women priests. Bridget pours this unmarried male priest's tea respectfully while Roberta offers him a large slice of heavily buttered wheaten bread.

'Well, Father,' begins Bridget, pushing up the half reading glasses on her nose with a friendly smile.

'We support you,' he says in a gentle Wexford accent, 'we are with you, we will help you—'

'Well, I hope so, Father,' interrupts Roberta. 'Bridget here's closer to the Virgin Mary than themuns in Magic Gory!'

After a momentary silence of deep embarrassment all-round the priest continues, 'We love you, we support you, we are with you, we will pray for you—'

'Aye, Father, but what exactly are youse goin' to *do*?' interrupts Patricia.

The gentle priest looks startled by the impertinence of these women's rude interruptions, and distributes multiple blessings as he promptly escapes to go to a more important meeting about the leak in the chapel roof. Wee Jack follows him up the street, licking crumbs from the turn-ups in his black trousers.

Another meeting ends in no meaningful offers of support for the GOGO Girls.

'I knew this wasn't goin' to be easy,' says Jean, 'but I was hopin' somebody would want to help us.'

'Don't give up, girls, it's early days,' says Bridget. 'And, sure, guess what? Haven't we been invited to the big Good Community Relations Conference in the Europa Hotel?'

'No way!' says Roberta.

Bridget hands a letter of invitation to Jean.

'It'll be comin' down with people wantin' to support our campaign.'

9

'Oh, it's dead swanky in here, so it is,' says Patricia.

'The only time I was ever in the Europa Hotel in my whole life was when my Derek brought me here for a chicken Maryland for our silver wedding anniversary,' says Jean, 'but there was a bomb scare halfway through the main course and we had to get out quick.'

'Ach, no, Jean,' says Patricia.

'Yes, Patricia, love, the Provos blew up the restaurant before my apple tart and fresh cream came. In all the fuss to get out I left my anniversary card on the table and God knows where it ended up because half the bloody restaurant landed in the middle of Great Victoria Street. There wasn't a windie left in the place, Patricia, and my Derek was ragin, so he was.'

'Oh, don't talk to me!' says Patricia.

It's only four years since Jean lost her Derek, and every day a happy memory of their life together returns she feels a familiar deep pang of pain. After all they had been through during the Troubles it still seemed unfair that Derek had been killed by a superbug in the City Hospital. Trevor had joked darkly that his father had escaped the Provos and the UVF, but it was the National Health Service that got him in the end. Jean didn't approve of Trevor's black sense of humour, although she thought sometimes that it might explain how he coped with Valerie and all her complaints.

Jean and Patricia are sitting in the front row at the annual Belfast Good Community Relations Conference in the Europa

Hotel. The GOGO Girls received their unexpected invitation to the event following Patricia's appearance on *The Nolan Show*. Wee Jack is home alone in Patricia's house for the first time since Isobel's death. He is shredding a plump cushion from Harry Corry's into hundreds of tiny pieces.

'The free lasagne and coleslaw was gorgeous at lunchtime, so it was,' says Jean.

'Aye, but the free lemon meringue was nathin' on yours, Jean, love,' assures Patricia.

'All this free grub's marvellous,' says Jean. 'No wonder Big Stan has a belly on him the size of Black Mountain!'

'Here comes that lovely big educated fella in the corduroys again,' says Patricia. 'This morning when he stood up at the front I loved all them big words he used about peace and coexisters and inter-places and all, and did you hear me shouting "hear, hear", Jean, when he said we should have a shared future?'

'Better than a scared future!' jokes Jean.

'Why's he wearing his bicycle clips over his cords, Jean?' asks Patricia.

'Well, he probably came here on his bike cos he's dead Green and all.'

'But that's not fair, Jean. For his job he's not supposed to be neither Green nor Orange.'

'Shh!' says an earnest woman from Queen's University in the row behind.

'I don't mean that sort of *green*. I mean he likes the environment like swanky people who eat birdseed up the Lisburn Road. He rides his bike to stop the climate changin', so he does.'

'Well, if he's a vegetarian, he probably needs to keep them clips on his cords, Jean, you know, just in case all them beans give him the runs!' says Patricia laughing.

'Ach, Patricia, you're a hoot, so you are,' says Jean, as the woman from Queen's University leans forwards again to shush the two giggling friends.

However their mirth ceases suddenly when they notice Big Stan from the Loyalist Interface Group and Wee Malachy from the Republican Interface Group walking to the front of the room to be greeted by a nice woman with make-up and a pearl necklace from the Good Community Relations Council. Jean and Patricia look on in shock as the eager woman assists the two men in preparing a presentation on a computer and a data projector.

'Look at that wee skitter Wee Malachy, all smiles, gettin' yer woman to stick his wee dingle into her laptop,' says Patricia.

'Tell me about it, love,' says Jean. 'You know I can't stand the way no one just talks to you any more. They always have to put fancy pictures up on the wall with their computers as if it makes it less borin'.'

'I bet this will be as borin' as bloody Brexit,' whispers Patricia.

'And our next Sustainable Good-Practice Shared-Space-Collaboration Presentation this afternoon,' says the lovely big educated fella with the corduroys and the big words, 'is from Stan of the Loyalist Interface Group and Malachy of the Republican Interface Group, who are going to tell us about their absolutely sterling work on the interface, a wonderful cross-community project in West Belfast between LIG and RIG.'

'LIG and RIG? Frig!' says Patricia.

The serious woman from Queen's ceases her copious note taking on her tablet computer to lean forwards and glare at Patricia. Jean and Patricia roll eyes, make a face, mouth 'thinks she is somethin'' to one another and then listen quietly as the two powerful community workers explain how they have been working together to build reconciliation across the peace wall for the past three years.

'Three years ago, as a result of the challenges we presented about the criminal neglect of our two communities by the Good Community Relations Council—' begins Wee Malachy.

'Absolutely,' agrees the lovely big educated fella repentantly.

'We received two hundred and fifty thousand pounds to …' continues Wee Malachy.

'Two hundred and fifty wha?' exclaims Jean, looking at an equally wide-mouthed Patricia.

'To employ community workers to …' continues Stan.

'Aye, jobs for the boys!' whispers Patricia.

The women are too shocked to listen to the presentation that follows. They don't hear anything about the strategic objectives and intended peacebuilding outcomes of the project. The explanation about capacity building and single identity work completely passes them by, and they miss the colourful graphs showing progress against key performance indicators entirely.

'Two hundred and fifty wha?' repeats Jean, rubbing her neck.

'I thought them two hated each other,' says Patricia, 'but it's amazin' what a few pounds can do.'

The two women just manage to tune in to the final few minutes of the presentation when Big Stan and Wee Malachy explain that the first three years was only a pilot, because the local people aren't ready for cross-community contact yet, and so they need funding for another three years of single identity, capacity-building work, before the two communities will be ready to start talking to each other about when they think they might be ready to talk to each other about the possibility of talks about taking the peace walls down, by mutual consent, with agreement, when everybody's happy, and no one's being forced into it by middle-class do-gooders from the leafy suburbs.

'Absolutely!' agrees the lovely big educated fella with the corduroys.

'Why does Wee Malachy want more money for a single identikit?' whispers Patricia.

'They just want to keep their jobs goin', love,' says Jean angrily, 'and neither of the two of them is a bloody bit interested in gettin' our gate open!'

'Shush!' says the woman from Queen's University. 'The literature suggests that a lot more primary and secondary research will be required before the interface barriers can be removed.'

'Shush, yerself, you and yer oul My Pad!' Patricia retorts.

The woman's mouth falls open. No one has ever spoken to her like this before – in all her years of studying the exclusion of marginalised women with low educational attainment on the interfaces of West Belfast. She cannot hide her disgust at the disrespect and ingratitude for the PhD she has worked so hard to earn to help people like this.

At the end of the presentation, after a warm round of applause and hearty congratulations for the two courageous peacebuilders and their remarkable key performance indicators, there is an opportunity to ask questions to draw on the great expertise of the two speakers. Jean raises her hand immediately.

'Yes, the woman in the pink anorak in situ in the front row,' points the lovely big educated man with the long words.

'Hello, I'm Jean from the GOGO Girls. I would like to ask Big Stan and Wee Malachy what they're gonna do to help our campaign to get the peace gate open—'

'MY COMMUNITY IS NAT READY FOR THAT YET!' reply Big Stan and Wee Malachy abruptly in complete unison. The two men are singing from the same hymn sheet.

An uncomfortable silence follows in the conference room and the nice woman with the pearls from the Good Community Relations Council raises an eyebrow.

Stan notices this response and staring at her adds, 'It's only middle-class do-gooders from leafy suburbs who don't live in my community who want the peace walls to come down.'

Another silence.

The lovely big educated fella with the long words coughs and attempts to rescue the situation by saying something about multiple deprivation differentials and community cohesion and generational change and the importance of government policy being fit for purpose and outcomes focused.

Eventually Wee Malachy gives an answer, looking at Big Stan for support, 'I've always said that weemin have a role in my community.'

'Absolutely!' says the nice educated fella, as one of his bicycle clips falls to the floor.

'RIG and LIG would be happy to help any weemin's group that wants to support our work,' adds Big Stan.

'Frig RIG and LIG!' whispers Patricia.

'Yes, of course,' says Wee Malachy. 'We are always lookin' for ways of gettin' new people involved in all our projects.'

'Aye, my arse,' whispers Jean, 'as long as you're related to him or in *his* organisation!' And then she addresses the conference delegates, 'Well, then, will youse two come together to our next meetin' to help us?'

Wee Malachy and Big Stan look at each other uncertainly. They are usually the ones who shake the status quo by speaking up on behalf of the residents and challenging the speakers at conferences like this. This is uncomfortable territory for men accustomed to government officials who are too afraid to ever challenge them.

'Ach, of course we will, Jean, love, sure, I've known you for years,' says Big Stan smiling.

'Next Wednesday then!' concludes Jean in the presence of one hundred and fifty good-community-relations witnesses.

The woman from Queen's University even notes it down on her tablet. 'I'd love to do a focus group with you some time,' she whispers, 'on the impact of feminism on the peace walls and clichéd representations of women like you in West Belfast.'

'Sorry, love, you can stick someone else under your microscope,' says Patricia.

At the end of the conference, Jean and Patricia are busy filling in evaluation forms on the event to let the funders know the food was nice and that the day wasn't a complete waste of time.

'Jean,' says Patricia, 'it says here – Did your attendance at the conference increase your knowledge, understanding and skills in peacebuilding and reconciliation? You can tick agree or disagree but there's no box for aye, my arse!'

Just then the lovely big educated fella arrives on the scene.

'Hello, love,' says Jean, 'I'm sorry we interrupted your nice presentation but we know what them two are really like. They're takin' you for a ride, son.'

'Absolutely!' he replies, taking the two women to the side. 'Listen, ladies, I can't say too much, but I'm in regular contact with senior loyalists and republicans and everyone is well aware of the issues. All I can say is that we're all working very hard to help those two out of the jungle, but it takes time.'

'How much time do they need?' says Jean. 'We've had over twenty years of peace nigh. I'm tellin' you, them two are full of shite.'

The leading authority on peace in Northern Ireland is stumped for a second, but then he has an idea. 'Listen, ladies,' he says, 'we are having a visit from a delegation of women from Rwanda next month and—'

'Oh, God!' says Patricia, 'isn't that where everyone died in the genocide?'

'Absolutely!' replies the lovely big educated fella, 'a million people died in a hundred days in the genocide in Rwanda in 1994, and for twenty-five years now people have been working on local community reconciliation over there.'

'Puts this place in perspective,' says Jean.

'Nightmare,' says Patricia, more quietly and thoughtfully than usual.

'There are ordinary women there, like you,' he explains, 'who have had the courage to work for a better future in their local communities too. Some of them are visiting Northern Ireland to learn about our peace process—'

'I bet they can't afford bloody peace walls in Rwanda,' says Patricia.

'So if you would like to meet some of the delegation, I can bring them to meet you.'

'Aye, son, that would be lovely,' says Jean, genuinely pleased to be recognised in this way.

'But you need to watch your bike up our way, son,' says Patricia, 'in case some wee hood nicks your wheels.'

'Absolutely!' says the lovely big educated fella smiling before noticing that his other bicycle clip has detached from his corduroys.

Jean and Patricia complete the rest of their evaluation forms with lots of ticks against 'excellent', and Patricia adds in the additional-comments box that 'the lasagne was gorgeous, so it was' and the two women depart from their first Good Community Relations Conference feeling good.

10

By the time Wednesday morning comes around the GOGO Girls are more nervous and defiant than ever.

'I've Wee Jack with me again the day,' announces Patricia, bursting through the doors of the cross-community pensioners' club meeting room with the late Isobel's Jack Russell on her lap in the wheelchair. 'He frets somethin' shockin' when I leave the house, the wee crater. He keeps thinkin' I'm gonna leave him for good like Big Isobel, God love him.'

'Well, don't let him near the cups and saucers again, Patricia, for God's sake!' says Bridget disapprovingly.

'Ach, Bridget, catch yerself on, he only wants a wee lick,' starts Patricia, but before an argument can develop the two powerful community leaders arrive together.

'Welcome back, gentlemen,' says Jean.

There is a certain amount of tension in the air as Bridget pours the tea for Big Stan and Wee Malachy. Both men firmly decline all offers of Roberta's rhubarb tart. There is little small talk and Wee Jack growls intermittently in the direction of the two men.

'Listen,' says Big Stan, 'we know your wee cross-community pensioners' lunches are brilliant, and everyone round here knows Wee Jean's pavlovas are legendary, but yousens need to be careful at your age, about gettin' involved in things youse know nathin' about.'

The women say nothing but their faces communicate what

they are thinking – patronising shite! This looks like it is going to be their shortest meeting yet. As Wee Malachy rises to leave he pats Bridget on the shoulder.

'So are you goin' to support our campaign or not?' asks Bridget.

'Don't worry, dear,' he whispers, 'I'll get your wee ideas put on the agenda of the next Cross-Community Leaders' Peace and Reconciliation Network Residential in the Slieve Donard Hotel. I'll let youse know what the men say.' Then winking, he promises, 'I'll get youse a bit of money for a Christmas dinner for all the pensioners and youse can do your cross-community Santa again if youse want.'

Bridget bristles and the two men leave quickly, explaining that they must go to an urgent meeting about demanding an extension to the funding for their communities so they can keep paying themselves their salaries. As they leave the women can hear the conversation between the two men in the corridor outside.

'They've no idea the amount of trouble we stop on this interface,' says Wee Malachy.

'That's the thanks you get,' says Big Stan.

Roberta is now pressing her ear against the door.

'Don't worry, they're harmless oul dolls,' says Wee Malachy. 'That gate will be opened when we decide.'

'Aye, sure we'll talk about it at the next meeting at the Slieve Donard,' says Stan.

The collective face of the GOGO Girls darkens dangerously.

'Them two's full of shite!' says Roberta as soon as the two community leaders are out of earshot.

'That Big Stan is a buck eejit!' says Jean.

'If they would just work together to take the peace wall down, the same way they're working together to keep their jobs,' says Bridget.

'Right, that's it!' says Patricia, who is about to explode.

Jean looks concerned.

'Them two with their LIG and their RIG can frig away off. I'm goin' to do something for myself!'

Bridget gasps. Patricia pulls the banner down from the wall and accelerates her wheelchair out the door. Wee Jack jumps off her lap with a yelp and follows close behind.

'Oh, fuckaduck!' says Roberta and puts her hand over her eyes.

Patricia erupts onto the street clutching the 'Get Our Gate Open' banner, accelerating her wheelchair belligerently. Wee Jack follows close behind and uses all the power his little legs can muster to keep up with the speeding wheelchair. The new four-legged resident of Patricia's household has already worked out when his boss means business. Wee Jack can sense when Patricia is happy and carefree and likely to shower him with biscuits from the tin in the kitchen cupboard beside the dog food. The wily mutt can also tell when to keep his head down, such as when Liam arrives home after dark, staggering and with a strange smell on his breath. It only took one experience of being splattered by a tub of cottage cheese bouncing off Liam's inebriated head for Wee Jack to learn to get offside during marital disputes.

As Wee Jack scampers in hot pursuit of his mistress, the rest of the GOGO Girls are peeking out from the front door of the church afraid of what is about to unfold.

Patricia swivels her wheelchair aggressively in a skilful three-hundred-and-sixty-degree turn and addresses her friends, 'That's it, girls – that's it! I'm not sittin' round beggin' no more bloody MEN for permission!'

Big Stan and Wee Malachy and their personal assistants, wearing denim jackets and having a smoke, have not yet departed and stand on the pavement looking on in amazement. With another three-hundred-and-sixty-degree swivel Patricia pirouettes her wheelchair and faces the peace gate. Jean, Roberta and Bridget look after her with a mix of fear, confusion and bemusement.

'Dear God, Bridget, her head's melted,' says Jean.

'Patricia, calm down now, love,' shouts Roberta, 'you'll give yourself a canary!'

But Patricia holds her wheelchair joystick and speeds directly towards the peace gate.

'I haven't seen her go that fast since the tickets went on sale for the Daniel O'Donnell concert in the Waterfront Hall!' cries Roberta.

The other women begin to follow, walking as fast as their painful hips and knee joints will allow.

'My hip's killing me,' winces Bridget. 'But just keep moving. She's taking the head staggers. You never know what she'll do when she goes off on one like this!'

Roberta cleans her glasses and watches anxiously as Patricia arrives at the pedestrian entrance to the peace gate. 'Oh, my God, what's she doin' now? Patricia is goin' plain friggin' "Loco in Acapulco"!'

An ice cream van is parked beside the peace gate and Seamie and Anto are standing in the queue. None of the customers appear to be buying ice cream. Once served they swiftly place the small packets they purchase into their pockets and depart quickly. Anto is the first to notice Patricia driving her wheelchair at speed towards the peace gate.

'Watch out, Seamie,' he shouts, pointing at Patricia, 'here comes fuckin' Davros!'

'Get outta my way, ya wee scumbegs!' yells Patricia. 'I've had enough of the whole bloody lotta youse!'

She points at Seamie and shouts, 'Look at that wee gabshite! His granda died for Ireland and all he can do is torture bloody pensioners!'

Seamie is taken aback at this targeted insult.

Cleverly using the joystick on her wheelchair, Patricia manoeuvres herself into the small pedestrian opening in the gate. She moves backwards and forwards in the opening until the wheelchair is completely stuck.

Jean is first to arrive at the gate, breathless and rubbing her chest, and she tries to get the wheelchair unstuck. 'Patricia, love, have you gone mad? Screamin' in the street like a banshee and nigh you're stuck!'

'It's this bloody country that's mad and stuck – not me,' shouts Patricia, unfurling the 'Get Our Gate Open' banner and raising it above her head as best she can. 'Youse can all bloody like it or lump it!' she shouts.

In a canine act of support Wee Jack lifts a leg and pees up the peace gate.

Seamie pockets the drugs he has just purchased from the ice cream van and, staring at Patricia, whispers to Anto, 'That oul doll must be on some of them too.'

Seamie and Anto join a growing crowd of spectators including Wee Malachy and several of his staff and Big Stan and Big Stan's driver. Roberta tries to move the wheelchair by turning around and heaving her backside against it again and again.

'Yer specky woman's fuckin' twerkin'!' mocks Seamie.

Roberta's glasses steam up with all the exertion, but no matter how hard she pushes the wheelchair remains stuck.

'Oh, Patricia, love, you're gonna get hurt!' she says.

Patricia cannot and will not be moved.

'I shall nat, I shall nat be moved!' she chants.

'Bridget, go and get Liam from the bookies to talk some sense into her,' says Jean.

'He's away fishin' in Toome the day with his worms,' Patricia states immediately, revealing that this action may not be as impulsive as it first appeared.

'Phone Stephen Nolan at the BBC and Paul Clark on the UTV and all themuns on that Sky News and tell them my protest has started!'

'Nightmare!' says Roberta.

Patricia seems to rise in her wheelchair as she addresses the assembled crowd. 'I am a disabled woman and this gate is not wide enough for my wheelchair for till get through. The whole world needs to know that this is discrima-bloody-nation!'

Wee Jack stands beside his mistress and repeatedly yaps a high-pitched bark as if it is dog language for 'Hear, hear!' 'Bravo!' and 'Go on, ya girl ye!'

Patricia takes a deep breath and continues, 'Yes, this is nothing short of discrimination against people with disabilities. My human rights are being abused. This gate should be open to let everyone through the peace wall the same. This is about equality! This gate discriminates against disabled people. I'm takin' this to the European Court of Human Rights.'

'But what about Brexit?' asks Roberta.

Patricia ignores Roberta and everyone else who has gathered in a small crowd beside the peace gate. 'Get our gate open!' she shouts. 'Get our gate open!'

Jean and Bridget heave against the back of the wheelchair and try once more to push Patricia through the gate, but they are running out of breath and it is clear their friend is completely and deliberately stuck in the peace wall.

'I shall nat, I shall nat be moved!
I shall nat, I shall nat be moved.
I'm like an MP sittin' on his big backside,
I shall nat be moved!'

'Oh, Jesus, Mary and Joseph,' says Bridget, now in more of a fluster than ever.

Patricia grabs her pink smartphone, takes a selfie of her stuckness and shares it on every social media outlet she can think of complete with the hashtag GOGO.

'There, it's on Instergram and Tweeter and BakeBook and everything nigh!' she shouts, waving her phone aggressively towards Big Stan and Wee Malachy.

The two men's mouths drop from bemusement to disbelief.

'We're not gonna get the gate opened this way,' frets Bridget.

Seamie whispers into Anto's ear, 'Them oul dolls had better watch themselves.'

Wee Jack growls as if he overhears Seamie's words in dog frequency.

'I know,' replied Anto. 'They think they're the Fantastic fuckin' Four.'

'We'll see about this! I've had it up to here with askin' permission from bloody useless men,' growls Patricia.

Bridget bends down and whispers into her friend's ear, 'Patricia, love, I never heard you ask Liam's permission for anything in your life. Come on, love, catch yourself on. You're going to make yourself bad with your nerves again.'

But Patricia is deaf with fury. She grabs her smartphone once again and hits a number on her speed dial. 'Hello? Is that the *Belfast Telegraph*? Get yourselves a photographer up here right nigh.'

11

A copy of the *Belfast Telegraph* is sitting on the table in the pensioners' meeting room. No one dares touch the newspaper and it is certainly the elephant in the room. No tea is being served. There is not the slightest suggestion that any tray bakes will be on offer this morning. The 'Get Our Gate Open' banner rests forlornly on the floor in the corner. So far no one has spoken a single word about the incident the day before.

Jean, Roberta and Bridget sit in sullen silence as Patricia fiddles sheepishly with the controls of her wheelchair, avoiding eye contact with everyone else in the room. Finally Bridget breaks the ice. She places her reading glasses on the end of her nose, pressing them firmly in place with her elegant forefinger and proceeds to read the newspaper headline while sternly looking over the top of her lenses in Patricia's direction.

'Disabled Pensioner Arrested For Wasting Police Time.'

'I've never been so scundered in all my life!' says Roberta. 'That was worse than when my wee windie cleaner fell off his ladder after he saw me cuttin' my toenails in my knickers through the bedroom windie!'

'Patricia, love,' begins Jean, softly, 'I know you meant well, but we need to be better organised than that.'

Bridget remains tight-lipped and simply stares at Patricia who does not reply to Jean but looks suitably ashamed. The day before it had taken three hours to extricate Patricia's wheelchair from the peace gate, in which time both the photographer from the *Belfast Telegraph* and the PSNI arrived to record the incident in full. The fire service were also called to the rescue. At first Patricia resisted the help of the brave firefighters.

'Here, Hugh, Pugh and Barney McGrew, listen to me – you can fuck away aff!' she shouted to the great shock of all concerned. 'Away and save a wee cat up a tree somewhere!'

With this behaviour she lost the support of half the onlookers. As a friendly policewoman drew near for a softly-softly approach, Patricia was having none of it.

'Oh, yes, youse can get your arses out of that police station of yours now to harass a poor disabled woman, but you couldn't even open the peace gate to let Big Isobel through in her coffin.'

'What medication is she on?' asked the policewoman sympathetically.

'She's nat on nathin', so she's nat, apart from a Bacardi and Coke at the weekends,' replied Roberta.

Patricia's selfie of being stuck in the peace gate had gone viral on Facebook but she received as many attacks from online trolls as supportive comments from well-wishers.

'Them bloody interweb trowels are doin' my head in, so they are, Jean, love,' she says. 'They won't leave me alone and I've never heard so much nasty bastardness in all my born days.'

'Well, love, you're playin' with fire on them oul internets and you're goin' about things all the wrong way,' says Jean, 'and I've told you before that you don't have to twitter out every bloody thing that comes into yer bap like Donald flippin' Trump.'

Wee Jack rests his chin on the arm of the wheelchair and looks around at the GOGO Girls one by one with big forlorn eyes. There is another minute of silence.

'Aye, but, here,' says Roberta eventually, 'wasn't thon big fireman that looked like yer man George Clooney, the one that cut her out of the gate, wasn't he just gorgeous with his teeth and his big arms and all?'

Patricia attempts a smile.

'I remember when I was a wee girl in the home,' says Roberta, 'Wee Lizzie Magee set fire to the curtains in the dining room after a swanky social worker told her she'd never amount to nathin'—'

'Oh, tell me no more,' says Bridget. 'I've heard enough about abuse in those homes to do me a lifetime.'

'Anyway,' interrupts Roberta, 'the next thing the fire brigade arrives, lights flashin' and everything, and me and Betty Cooper get carried down the stairs by a big fireman with a lovely moustache and all. The firemen were dead nice, so they were, and they brought us toys to the home on Christmas Eve and I got my first Cindy doll and game of ludo.'

After a momentary extension of uneasy silence, Jean stifles a quiet chuckle. 'Says you to that big fireman that looked like yer man George Clooney, Patricia, "Ya know, son, I had lovely legs like my mother and Rita Hayworth when I had them."'

Bridget can't help but join in the chuckle as Roberta continues, 'I had a wee feel of his big muscles when we were helpin' him carry Patricia over to the police car. Brought me right back, so it did!'

Soon all the women, including Patricia herself, begin to laugh. 'Oh, listen to the ha has of her and the he hes of me!' cries Patricia.

Finally Wee Jack completes the scene with an outburst of joyful barking and eventually the GOGO Girls cannot stop laughing. When the laughter stops the mood becomes more serious, and without a word the women turn together and raise the 'Get Our Gate Open' banner aloft once more.

12

'Yes, love, it's a repeat prescription for my angina,' says Jean on the phone. 'Thanks very much, I'll pick it up this afternoon when I'm in for my corns.'

It's a week later and Jean is once again walking towards the peace gate, carrying a heavy bag of shopping. Since the corner shop in her street was demolished Jean's nearest grocery shop is on the other side of the peace wall. She pops in regularly as there is a much longer walk to the nearest supermarket on her own side of the wall. Jean is pragmatic when it comes to the sectarian divisions in Belfast. She is just as happy in a Catholic shop as in the Protestant shop, as long as the prices are the same. Of course, they didn't sell the Queen's Golden Jubilee mugs in the Catholic corner shop, but someone once won ten thousand pounds on the Lotto there and they always have a great offer on Galtee streaky bacon.

She is a little distracted as she shuffles along. Today she's thinking about her Trevor and that Valerie, and her wee Darren out in Afghanistan. She's worried about her chest pains at night and the squeak on the hinge of the kitchen cupboard. But most of all she is thinking about how the GOGO Girls can recover from Patricia's ill-fated publicity stunt and start to plan the next steps to get the peace gate opened.

Jean struggles with the shopping bag. The older she gets the heavier it becomes – and her knee is playing up today. The bag contains all her favourites: a carton of full-cream milk (none of that oul semi-skimmed nonsense), a tin of baked beans, a plain loaf, two soda bread and two potato bread farls for a nice fry at the weekend, a box of Tunnock's tea cakes, half a dozen eggs and a packet of bargain streaky bacon. As she limps towards the pedestrian opening in the peace gate she notices Seamie loitering as usual. The troubled young man is once again standing on the street corner, slouching and smoking with his hood up. Jean has thought about him quite a few times since their recent encounters. She can't decide whether she needs to fear him or help him, but on this occasion she instinctively feels for the purse in her pocket and clasps it tightly. In her nervousness, as she approaches the young man, Jean loses her usual sure-footedness and trips over some debris left behind from the previous night's stone throwing.

'Oh, here!' she cries as she begins to topple over.

When she falls, all her groceries spill out of the shopping bag and spread across the pavement like the contents of a recently firebombed Co-op during the Troubles. Seamie rushes forwards immediately. Jean cowers on the ground, placing one arm across her head to protect herself from the expected blows, still holding firmly onto her purse in her pocket with the other hand. Noticing this unexpected reaction, Seamie stops dead in his tracks.

'I was comin' to help ye!' he says indignantly. The offended young man scowls but he continues to help Jean to her feet.

'Sorry, love,' says Jean, 'I thought you were goin' to—'

'Nick your shappin'?' says Seamie with an affronted sniff. 'Do you think I would mug an oul doll like you for a bax of fuckin' Tunnix mallas?'

Despite the misunderstanding, Seamie starts to pick up Jean's groceries, including the aforementioned, and now somewhat squashed, box of fucking Tunnock's tea cakes, and carefully loads everything back into her shopping bag.

This is not the first time an older person has assumed the worst about Seamie because of how he looks. It seems his appearance, his age and where he comes from are all good reasons for strangers to fear him. He's used to it, and in some ways feels he deserves it, but he had started to like this old woman from the wrong side of the wall.

Without looking up he asks quietly, 'Is that what you think a wee scumbag would do, missus?'

Jean attempts a lie. 'No, son, I was just scared after fallin' and all. This new knee of mine has been givin' me awful gyp, so it has.'

'Aye, right,' sniffs Seamie.

He hands Jean her restored shopping bag.

'Now, do you want to search me for stolen tatty farls, missus?' he asks sarcastically, holding up his arms in surrender before he turns to walk away.

'C'mere, son,' says Jean. 'What's your name again anyway?'

The young man stops. There is something so kind in this old woman's voice. It reminds him of his grandmother's voice and he only vaguely remembers her. She had died during his first week at primary school. He recalls the wake and the funeral and his mother drinking away her grief for months. In fact, she is still drinking away her grief.

'Seamie.'

Jean holds out her hand. 'I'm Jean.'

Seamie scans the surrounding streets for a second to see if anyone is watching, but there is no sign of anyone and Anto has gone to the novena with his mammy. Seamie shakes Jean's hand.

'Do you not have a job, son?' she asks.

'I do labourin' for my Uncle Danny, but no one round here has any money for doin' up houses no more.'

'Do you not have a trade, son?' asks Jean.

'Well, I wanna go to the tech and do bricklaying,' answers Seamie.

Jean smiles broadly at this revelation. 'Well, you could do worse, son.' She beams and pats him on the back and says, 'My

Derek was a brickie all his days. It's a good trade for a young fella like you to be doin'. Sure, there's always goin' to be walls.'

For just a second Seamie and Jean raise their eyes to the peace wall towering over them. They look at each other and smile. Then, with this new-found common interest in bricklaying, Seamie raises his eyebrows slightly, drops the sides of his mouth and pouts in appreciation.

'Your oul lad must have been a good brickie, then?'

'The best in Belfast!' says Jean. 'He built half the council houses on the Shankill Road.'

Instinctively Seamie takes one handle of Jean's shopping bag and Jean takes the other and they walk together towards the gate.

'Are you alright, missus?' asks Seamie.

'Aye, son, I've had much worse scrapes than that in my day,' replies Jean.

When they reach the pedestrian opening Jean looks up at Seamie. 'Thanks very much, love. I'm sorry for … you know.'

Seamie hands Jean the whole shopping bag and helps her through the gap.

'Aye, I know, Jean,' he says softly.

As Jean is about to disappear through the gate back to the other side, she turns around. 'Here, Seamie, son, have you ever taken out an oul, done workin' kitchen?' she asks.

Seamie's eyes light up and he smiles. 'Oh, aye, missus. You should see me with a sledgehammer!'

13

'Yes, Valerie, you just need a stronger ointment to put on it, and make sure you rub it in and you'll be alright, love. Now stop worrying yourself, will ye?'

Jean is once again alone in her kitchen standing beside the pictures of her beloved family, talking on the telephone. She's used to being lonely now, but today she is missing Derek desperately. She wants nothing more than to see him in his chair having a wee smoke and shouting just one more time at some hapless politician on the lunchtime news. She dreams of just one more bank holiday trip to Newcastle for a poke and a wee dander on the beach where the Mountains of Mourne sweep down to the sea, followed by a quick go on the one-armed bandit and a vinegary fish supper. She sometimes daydreams of her last day out with Derek to the Auld Lammas Fair in Ballycastle for a picnic on a tartan blanket with a flask of hot tea, tomato sandwiches and wee paper bags of dulse and yellow man.

'Well, Bridget says you're better stickin' with paracetamol and not to take an antibiotic unless you're really despurt …'

When she's feeling lonely she sometimes telephones Valerie to ask about her ailments and to see how Trevor is getting on. Valerie is not the daughter-in-law she would have chosen for her only son. Her haughtiness and hypochondria are hard to bear at times, but she's a good mother and it's clear she loves Trevor, and her big son adores Valerie. As long as my Trevor's happy, she thinks every time Valerie says or does something that jars with Jean's sense of what a good wife should be.

In recent years she has become more tolerant of her daughter-in-law's foibles, particularly the more she has got to know Valerie's own mother. 'Our Valerie's hard work,' Jean once confided to Bridget, 'but, dear God, you should listen to her ma with the yappy poodle in that bloody perfect detached bungalow with the white windie shutters in Bangor.'

Unfortunately it's that time of the night at that time of the year when Jean can hear the sound of sectarian abuse and bricks being hurled across the peace gate outside her house. It's so normal that Jean usually just goes into the back room and turns up *Emmerdale* but today she wishes it would stop in case Valerie hears it.

'I know, Valerie, love, but you know our Trevor would just love to come home, and I'm sure the bank would give him a transfer.'

A flying bottle smashes against the peace wall outside.

'But, Jean, darling, you know Trevor loves it over here in England, and you know only too well that those dissident republicans are still targeting our security forces, and it's easier for me to get a prescription over here, even if I do have to pay for it,' Valerie chatters.

'Well, I know, Valerie, love, but it's not as bad over here now as it was when yousens left, and c'mere till I tell ye, that shower in Westminster are no better than our buck eejits up at Stormount. Sure look at the Horlicks they've made over Brexit – they're startin' to make Northern Ireland look sensible! What, love?'

Jean covers the mouthpiece of the phone and turns away from the front of the house in case her daughter-in-law can detect the increasing volume of recreational rioting from the street. Glancing out the kitchen window at the rear of the house she notices that bloody magpie at the bins again and gives the window a rap to shoo away the nuisance.

'Och, that's just the TV, love. Some oul American *CSI* thing or somethin'.'

'Jean, do you think I'm stupid?' starts Valerie. 'Mummy says with Brexit there's going to be a United Ireland and they're not a bit happy about it in the golf club in Bangor, and they can't agree on anything up in Stormont, and I know rightly those young reprobates are still rioting outside your house right now.'

'Well, yes, I know they still do, but they're only youngsters with nathin' better to do.'

Jean sits down, rubbing her chest and starts to plead, 'Sure, you and Trevor could afford a nice big house in Newtownards nigh. They're goin' for next to nathin' since that oul recession and all, and you should see the lovely coffee shops in the town, Valerie, love. You can have a flat cappuccino every couple of shops nigh, and you should see that gorgeous Victoria Square. It has all them beautiful swanky shops you love, and if you and Trevor want to have more kids, and you're not past it yet, and I'm not puttin' you under any pressure, but I'll pay for them to get a tutor to make sure they get the eleven-plus, and you know the grammar schools over here are very, very good and you don't have to pay for a good school like you do over there— '

There is a knock at the front door.

'Here, I'd better go, Valerie, love,' says Jean, as the letter box rattles. 'There's the door. You go to bed with that head of yours and tell that big son of mine to do your ironin' and make you a nice cup-a-tay.'

Jean hangs up the phone and leaves the kitchen briefly. She returns with a blank envelope in her hand. This is the second mysterious envelope she has received this month – the first being Big Isobel's legacy. She opens the letter, half expecting another pleasant surprise like the one from Big Isobel's solicitor. She reads the four words cut out from a newspaper and glued onto the single sheet of plain white paper: 'GATE STAYS CLOSED BITCH.'

Jean gasps and sits down in shock, crumpling the note in her hand and holding her chest.

14

Jean knocks on the door of a red-bricked terrace house in Eccles Street, on the other side of the Shankill Road, and waits patiently. She knows it will take a while for Wee Bertie to make it all the way from his well-padded armchair to the front door. While she waits Jean looks down to check her stockings haven't gathered too much at the ankles, and she notices the front doorstep of this house is in need of a good scrub.

'God, love him,' she thinks, 'if Wee Bertie got down there to bleach his front step at his age, he might never get up again.'

Bertie Thompson is one hundred and two years old and reputedly the oldest man on the Shankill Road. As a veteran of Dunkirk in the Second World War he has universal approval on the Road. Even the paramilitaries dare not criticise him, although Bertie expresses plenty of uncensored criticism of them.

'I didn't fight the Nazis to have this Road controlled by drug dealers and gabshites who've never done a proper day's work in their lives,' he would say at the Remembrance Day parade.

As a young man Bertie had been a stretcher-bearer in both the Belfast Blitz and on the Dunkirk beaches. During the Troubles he was an ambulance driver, often arriving on the scene of the latest atrocity while the blood was still flowing. Today Bertie is still active and dresses immaculately in tweed blazer, military tie and beige trousers for his weekly trip to the British Legion. An old-fashioned bachelor, he lives alone, independently, in the house where he was born. His senses have barely dimmed, although a hearing aid and bottle-top glasses are of great assistance nowadays.

'He's still as sharp as a blade,' Roberta says. 'There's no sign of that oul fella goin' demental.'

In his nineties Bertie relented and began to use a walking stick in public for the first time. For his hundredth birthday there was a whip-round in the Legion to buy him a blackthorn stick with a gold-plated engraving: *To the Oldest and Wisest Man on the Shankill.*

He's grasping this blackthorn stick as he opens the door to Jean. 'Och, Wee Jean Beattie, Geordie's wee girl!' he says. 'Would you look at the cut of you, you're looking powerful well, so you are.'

Jean gives Bertie a kiss on the cheek.

'You're not looking so bad yerself, Bertie,' Jean replies. 'You don't look a day over ninety!'

'Come on in, love, and I'll make us a cup-a-tay,' says Bertie.

Inside Bertie's house is like a trip back in time. The furniture and the curtains haven't changed much since the 1950s, and the walls are covered in woodchip wallpaper from the 1970s with many layers of emulsion paint in different hues of beige added over the decades. 'Sure, it'll do me my time,' Bertie has been saying for the past forty years.

'Well, tell me this, Bertie,' begins Jean cheerfully, 'are you still seein' your girlfriend?'

Bertie smiles. 'Still goin' strong, Jean, love. I don't care what they're saying about me goin' with a woman twenty years younger, me and Dorothy are very happy, so we are.'

'Sure, eighty-two's not that much younger nowadays, love,' says Jean.

'We're going on the train for a day trip to Bangor next week,' explains Bertie excitedly, as if it's his first rather than thousandth such trip. 'Dorothy's makin' the sandwiches and I'm bringin' a nice flask of tea, and we'll sit and have a picnic at Pickie like in the good old days.'

'Lovely!' says Jean.

'Now, Jean, enough about this old romantic. What's this I hear about you being threatened over this whole gate thing?'

Jean takes the threatening note from her anorak pocket and shows it to Bertie.

'Oh, I've seen plenty of those in my time,' he says, as he scans the threatening message.

'Scared the life out of me, Bertie,' says Jean.

'That's what the cowards who do this want, Jean, love,' says Bertie.

'Oh, I know, Bertie. Sure, look at what happened to my Derek.'

'I remember it well, Jean, and your Derek was a good man too. He built walls to make safe homes for wee families, not walls to keep neighbours apart and loyal to the big men on their own side. You and those weemin from the other side are doing the right thing to say you want the walls down. Sure, we've had peace now for more than twenty years. It's pure laziness that's keepin' up them walls, if you ask me. Do we really need a thirty-foot wall to protect us because we're scared of stones from wee skitters?'

'I know, Bertie, it's hardly Dunkirk, and you would know,' says Jean.

Bertie stops for a moment and closes his eyes. 'I remember after the war when they built the Berlin Wall. I remember thinking that's not the answer for the German people, and I knew in my heart that one day it would come down. Well, I'm glad I lived to see that wall fall and, sure, now it's long gone. So why on earth do we still need a wall to separate good people in West Belfast? We used to live together round here, Jean, you mind, don't you? My people lived in Lanark Street with Catholics either side of them for years – good neighbours, all for their families. Good Belfast people. Does this latest crowd up at Stormount want us divided forever?'

'What should I do, Bertie?'

Bertie raises his bushy white eyebrows. 'I think you already know, without asking me, Jean.'

Jean pauses for a few minutes while Bertie holds the silence. Then she gently nods to herself.

'I can't go back now, Bertie. Sure, that would be worse than never having started the GOGO Campaign in the first place.'

Bertie takes Jean's hand. She notices how his skin feels soft, delicate and warm.

'There's no turning back when good people find their voice,' says Bertie.

'Oh, I don't know, Bertie. Maybe I should just shut up and go to bingo and leave it to the youngsters.'

'You're not going to do that, Jean Beattie. I know you're not. You weren't reared to be a pushover. Ah, Wee Geordie would be proud of you.'

Jean tears up at the words of this wise old man.

He looks into her soul with his ancient eyes. 'You're the same as me, Jean, so you are,' he says. 'You're a helper. You know, love, in this world there's talkers and takers and there's stirrers and shitesters, and they cause all the trouble. I saw it in the war and I've seen it here all my life in Belfast. I've watched it on this very street. But there are always helpers, Jean. No one remembers them, but it's the helpers, like you and me, in the background, who clean up the mess that others make with all their oul selfishness and hatred.'

Jean sits quietly for a moment. She feels a renewed sense of peace and purpose. 'You're right, Bertie,' she says. 'Sure, you're always right, so you are!'

'Well, I wasn't right for this year's Grand National,' says Bertie laughing. 'Dorothy nearly took the blackthorn to me for puttin' half my pension on the wrong bloody horse!'

Jean laughs along and stands up. 'Well, I'll not keep you, Bertie. I'm sure you're due a wee nap, love,'

'Houl your horses, Jean,' says Bertie. 'I've somethin' more pleasant in an envelope for you.'

Bertie gets up slowly, shuffles across the room and takes a small envelope from a drawer in his old mahogany sideboard. He hands it to Jean and when she opens the envelope inside she finds a small picture postcard of an old Irish bridge.

'My mother, God love her, bought me this postcard on our final holiday to Donegal in 1969, when she was on her last legs,' he explains. 'It's said to be the oldest bridge in Ireland, built by monks nearly a thousand years ago.'

Jean gazes at the yellowing picture postcard.

'We were stayin' in Bundoran and the reports on RTÉ about all that was goin' on back home were terrible. The British army was puttin' up barriers to stop the riotin' between the Falls and the Shankill. My mother was distraught at all the walls goin' up between friends and neighbours – she remembered the peace lines they put up in Belfast in the 1930s. And so on the day we visited the old Abbey Mill in Ballyshannon, she bought me this postcard and I'll never forget what she said to me, Jean. She said, "Just you remember, son. This bridge, built with love, has lasted a thousand years. Them walls they're puttin' up in Belfast, built in hate, will all fall down."'

'Thanks, Bertie, love,' says Jean, placing the postcard carefully into her handbag. 'You're a wee gem on this Road, so you are,' she says. 'I don't know what we'd do round here without you.'

'Thanks, Jean,' he replies. 'Now you look after yourself and that wee crater Roberta, won't you?'

'I will indeed, Bertie,' says Jean as she waves goodbye, 'and I'll come round and bleach that front step of yours the marra.'

15

The ice cream van is parked beside the peace gate again but there is no sign of the sale of a solitary ninety-nine. Today Sam and Lee are in the queue. Even though a notice on the rear of the van says *Watch Out for Children* there are no children in the queue and none of the customers are interested in buying ice cream.

The arrival of an ice cream van on a Belfast street is usually a moment of joy. Children rush to their parents begging for a few pounds for a poke or a screwball tub with a ball of bubblegum at the bottom of a plastic carton of synthetic ice cream. But this is clearly no ordinary ice cream van, and everyone (apart from the PSNI, apparently) knows it. In the past few months a darkness has descended upon this particular mobile merchandising operation. Even the dogs in the street know that the customers of this ice cream van are more interested in purchasing coke than a poke. There is a peculiar cross-community silence on challenging the shady proprietor with the dark sunglasses who some say keeps a few secrets about local community leaders on both sides of the peace wall. Every failing by the council, the Housing Executive, the NHS and the police is confronted aggressively by the leadership of LIG and RIG, but there is a lack of outrage regarding this major health issue affecting their communities.

Big Stan from the Loyalist Interface Group arrives in his black taxi. Everyone knows when this vehicle arrives on their street that important business is about to be conducted. Any teenager who has been complained about by a resident or one of Stan's relatives knows they should scarper long before the strong and tattooed arm above the law arrives to dispense justice. Big Stan motions to his driver to decelerate as he winds down the window and stares at the ice cream man who acknowledges Big Stan over his Armani sunglasses, smirks, dispenses a final packet and slowly drives off with the tune of 'I'm Popeye the Sailor Man' tinkling innocently through the loudspeakers on top of the vehicle.

'Let's get outta here,' says Lee.

'I hate them paramilitary bastards,' says Sam. 'The biggest hypocrites on this Road.'

'You leave my da out of it,' replies Lee.

'Ballicks!' says Sam.

Sam and Lee swiftly place the small packets they have just purchased into their pockets and run across the road to get into a Ford Focus with a broken window on the driver's side. At this very moment Jean, clutching the envelope with the threatening note, and Roberta are striding across the road towards the peace gate, and notice the two teenagers driving off at speed.

'Them wee lads are up to no good again,' says Jean. 'That's some poor crater's wee hatchback they've nicked in the town and they're goin' to go now and joyride the hell out of it and wreck it, the wee blurts, and someone's gonna lose their no-claims bonus and them wee lads don't give a damn!'

'Stop you upsetting yourself, Jean, love,' says Roberta. 'Sure, look, isn't that great to see?'

'What, love?' asks Jean.

Roberta points in the direction of the departing ice cream van. 'Well, at least the poke man is selling sliders till both sides nigh.'

'Aye, right nuff,' says Jean, rolling her eyes.

'During the Troubles there were always Catholic poke men

and Protestant poke men!' rejoices Roberta. 'Sure, there were Catholic bread men and Protestant bread men and even Catholic milkmen and Protestant milkmen. Sure, it was safer to get your food from your own side, so it was, but, sure, we've peace nigh, and, no, I know it's nat perfect, so it's nat, but it's a lot better than how things used to be round here, and, Jean, I'm fillin' up cos the childer are havin' wee cross-community pokes nigh—'

'They're selling friggin' drugs, Roberta! Will you catch yerself on!' interrupts Jean from the end of her tether.

Roberta is genuinely shocked. 'You mean the poke man is selling heroines and not ninety-nines?'

'Roberta, love, I may be Cagney, but you're no bloody Lacey,' says Jean.

'Nightmare!' says Roberta.

Big Stan approaches the two women and interrupts the conversation with an assured rudeness that has come from years of unchallenged bullying.

'I just wanted to let you know that my community did nat sanction them threats against youse weemin,' he proclaims.

'How do you know about it?' asks Roberta. 'Are you Mystic Meg or somethin'?'

Jean looks unconvinced, attempts a weak smile and walks on.

No one walks away from Big Stan.

'Listen, love, if we find out which of them wee hoods done it, we'll get their fuckin' ankles broke,' says Big Stan.

Now Jean halts and turns around. 'Don't you even think about hurtin' any children over this,' says Jean. 'No wonder the kids round here hate you and your so-called organisation.'

Oh, God, Jean, don't be sayin' that to him, thinks Roberta, dragging Jean along by the arm before she says anything further to upset Big Stan.

But Jean is in full flow now. 'So how many years is it nigh we've had peace? And youse boys still think youse can control everyone round here. Who gives youse the right to beat up childer for antisocial behaviour and drugs when youse are up to yer necks in it yourselves!'

Big Stan is speechless. No one speaks to him likes this. Everyone says it to each other but never to his face.

'Oh, Jean, love,' whispers Roberta, dragging her away, 'come on nigh, you're just upset with that oul note and Big Isobel's funeral and Cliff Richard not comin' to Belfast for Christmas this year—'

'I'm not afraid of him!' replies Jean, just loud enough for Big Stan to hear.

Roberta shuffles Jean along and leads her through the pedestrian opening in the peace gate and on towards the entrance to the church hall. Big Stan remains rooted to the pavement where he received Jean's missive. He has a look of disbelief on his face that turns to a flash of anger.

When Roberta feels they are at a safe distance, emboldened by Jean's challenge to the powers that be, she plucks up the courage to cast her own challenge in Big Stan's direction. 'It's a blinkin' disgrace!' she barks across the wall, and disappears into the church hall, breathing a sigh of relief as she slams the door behind them.

When Jean and Roberta arrive breathless into the cross-community pensioners' club room they find Bridget and Patricia sitting at the table looking at two notes with the same threatening message: GATE STAYS CLOSED BITCH.

Roberta is taken aback. 'Why did I nat get one?' she asks indignantly. 'I want the gate open too!'

Jean looks seriously at the other women. 'I don't know about yousens,' she says, 'but this just makes me even more determined.'

'I'm scared, Jean,' says Roberta.

'Aye, they're very brave fellas threatening old women!' says Bridget.

'Aye, but was it wee fellas who don't know any better or the big fellas who rule the roost round here?' says Jean. 'There's a hell of a difference, Bridget.'

'Are we goin' to phone the PSNI?' asks Roberta.

'Now what good would that do?' asks Patricia. 'Sure, them boys do this all the time and they never get caught.'

'Aye, and the peelers know rightly who does it,' adds Jean, 'but they go easy on them because they don't want to annoy them too much in case it's going to upset the peace process and all.'

'Sure, the peelers even tell the community leaders before they do a search for drugs in the estate, so as not to upset the community, and then the paramilitaries just move the drugs before the peelers even arrive!' says Roberta.

'Well, I had a chat with Wee Bertie the other day,' says Jean, 'and it's just made me more determined than ever.'

'Och, he's a wee dote, that wee man. I love him,' says Roberta. 'He fought for our freedom on the beaches in Duncairn!'

Patricia has had enough and grabs her phone. Bridget looks a little nervous.

'I tell you what, girls. No wee gabshite's gonna stop me doin' what I wanna do on my own road. I'm puttin' it on my BakeBook and we'll see how many likes it gets and then I'm phonin' Stephen Nolan and then we'll see who the big boys are around here!'

'Yes, but calm down a minute, Patricia, we need to get more people round here on our side first,' says Bridget.

'Patricia, houl your whisht for once!' says Jean.

The women think quietly for a few moments. Wee Jack looks around the group, curious about the silence. Then Jean has a light-bulb moment.

'Okay,' she announces, 'why don't we do a wee questionnaire round all the doors and see how many of the neighbours want the gate opened too? Them boys can't say their communities don't want the gate open if we've done a survey that shows that most people who live round here say they do want it open. How could they argue about that? All they ever say is that they represent the community.'

'It's dead funny, like, nobody came round the doors to ask us if we wanted the peace wall to go up in the first place,' says Patricia.

'Well, I think a questionnaire round the doors is a good idea, Jean,' says Bridget smiling. 'That way we all get a say, the ordinary residents, including the women, and not just the usual big mouthpieces on both sides.'

Bridget may give the impression she's a quietly spoken and modest old woman, but her friends know well that she has a spine of steel. Her husband, Gerard, had been a leading light in St Vincent de Paul throughout the Troubles, raising money and providing help for the poorest families in the community, even working quietly across the peace lines. Working alongside Gerard, Bridget saw and heard the worst of the suffering, grief and poverty in West Belfast during the darkest of years. On one occasion Gerard had received a threatening note for providing money to clothe the children of an informer who the IRA had tortured to death and dumped in a lane on the border. Gerard did not cower under this anonymous menace and went straight to the local Sinn Féin office with the sinister note and asked the most powerful man in his community politely but firmly, 'Is it true I'm going to have my head blown off for giving clothes to a dead tout's wee children? How's that a threat to Ireland?' Bridget was convinced it was the courage and tone of the questions that ensured the threat was never carried out.

The women are still nodding knowingly as Bridget continues, 'Then we can invite some more big important people along to our meetings and tell them what the people round here really want to happen. They'll listen to us more if we have hard evidence of community support.'

The women nod in firm agreement.

'There's no such word as *can't*,' says Roberta.

'Right, GOGO Girls!' says Jean defiantly. 'Here we go!'

She stands up and dramatically rips her threatening note into tiny pieces. Then the other two women stand up and ceremonially tear up their threats too. Wee Jack jumps from Patricia's lap onto the scattered paper and continues with an earnest destruction of the nasty notes, shaking his little head from side to side ferociously as the torn paper is decimated. The women shake their heads and laugh as if they cannot believe what they are doing.

'Oh, if my Derek could see me now,' says Jean giggling, 'he'd die laughin' in his grave!'

'Och, you're a hoot, Jean!' says Bridget laughing.

'Oh, my nerves!' shrieks Roberta.

The women link arms around the table and begin to sing together once again.

'Here we go, GOGO Girls, here we go,
here we go, GOGO Girls, here we go-o,
here we go, GOGO Girls, here we go,
here we go-o, here we go ...'

16

A feeling of excitement pervades the peace line, like on the days leading up to a parade and a protest. The Get Our Gate Open Campaign has begun in earnest. Big Stan has a heated conversation with Jean on why he was not consulted about the questions being asked in the consultation survey.

'My community did nat ask for no consultation,' he says.

'Well, I live in this community, Stan, and it's my community too, and I've been livin' here longer than you, so I have, and I want to ask my neighbours what they want and what they don't want, and when was the last time you asked anyone anything? So you can like it or lump it.'

'Listen, Jean, love,' begins Stan, attempting a more reasonable approach for a change, 'we got a grant to do a community audit for the new millennium and most people said they wanted the peace walls to stay up, so you're wasting your time.'

'Sure, that was years ago, Stan,' replies Jean without hesitation. 'People can change their minds, you know. What would your funders say if they knew you haven't asked the residents' opinions for near twenty years? Imagine if someone told them?'

This challenge is so effective that Big Stan relents and permits Jean to use one of his computers to prepare the survey in one of the offices in his community centre. A secret high-level meeting takes place between LIG and RIG in the rooftop bar of the Grand Central Hotel where Big Stan and Wee Malachy agree that to actively oppose the GOGO Girls might affect the next joint funding application for their salaries, and so a strategy of begrudging support is adopted in the certain knowledge that all the women's do-gooding nonsense will fail anyway. Wee Malachy allows Bridget to use the photocopier in his community centre to produce all the surveys and doesn't charge a penny for the paper and ink.

'That will help with the underspend in our Peace grant,' he explains.

Bridget shows admirable self-control by not sharing her immediate thought – it must be a very big underspend because you don't do any blessed peace work!

For two weeks the GOGO Girls go door to door carrying clipboards with their residents' survey. They leave additional questionnaires in all the well-frequented locations on both sides of the community: the doctor's surgeries, the dentists, the vets, the corner shops, the pubs and the bookies. Even the LIG and RIG community centres make the surveys available on request with the generous offer of personal assistance from Big Stan and Wee Malachy to help residents complete the questionnaire 'properly'. Bridget raises an eyebrow at this news.

Only the Free Presbyterian church on one side and the women's group run by Wee Malachy's wife on the other side refuse to take any surveys, both citing the same reason: they don't take a political position. On hearing this news Patricia's pencil-drawn eyebrows are raised to a millimetre off her scalp.

As the women progress around the streets of West Belfast, Patricia proudly balances a large pile of completed questionnaires on her lap, leaving no room for Wee Jack, who follows close behind wagging his tail. However, the biscuit treats are taking their toll and Wee Jack has developed a little pot belly and a slight waddle. If his tummy gets any bigger, it risks skirting the ground.

'You're spoiling that wee dog rotten,' points out Bridget.

'Och, sure he's his mammy's wee man, so he is, aren't you,

Jack?' replies Patricia, reaching down and tickling Wee Jack's pot belly defiantly.

This is the busiest Patricia has been in years. It reminds her of the happy days she spent working in the shirt factory before the Troubles and before she lost her legs in the bomb. No one but Liam really knows the pain and heartache Patricia experienced because of her injuries. Not even Bridget. Patricia kept up a brave face in public, but in private she shed many tears for all she had lost. Only Liam knows the depths of her despair, especially in the early days when Patricia felt she could not go on living with such a disability. Liam had heard the whole story and no one else knew what comfort and strength he had been to his dear wife. Everyone in the street thought Liam was just a useless big crater and Patricia was great craic despite all she had been through. Patricia often referred to Liam as 'a stupid oul blurt' and sometimes the neighbours dismissed Patricia as 'a bit of a looper', but no one knew the whole story of their pain, the extent of their resilience and the depth of their love for one another.

As the consultation with residents on the removal of the peace gate continues, a few setbacks threaten to derail the process. Wee Malachy informs Bridget that if most people in his community say they want the gate removed, he would need to carry out another survey to see if they really meant it.

'Bridget, love, I'm glad to see you weemin gettin' involved in the community,' he says, 'but you have to be careful you're nat bein' used by the Brits.'

The patronising tone and unspoken threat of this comment triggers memories of the way the powers that be used to speak to her Gerard during the Troubles. A family man involved in the church with no paramilitary connections, the likes of Wee Malachy didn't regard him as a true Irishman in the struggle against British oppression. To Bridget, her Gerard was the real man, putting faith and life and family before politics and power and nationalism. The memory emboldens her.

'What have the Brits go to do with it, Malachy?' enquires Bridget. 'Sure, they went home years ago. I haven't seen a Brit in my front garden for nearly thirty years!'

Wee Malachy begins his explanation, speaking slowly and deliberately as if suggesting that Bridget lacks the intellect required to understand the reality of Irish politics. 'Clearly the British government want us to think all the problems round here are about sectarianism and two communities that can't live together when clearly we all know the biggest problem is the continued presence of British imperialism in Ireland.'

'Don't be dressing it up in politics, Malachy,' replies an angry Bridget. 'If you don't want those Protestants from over there next nor near you, at least be honest enough to say it!'

As the surveying continues, Seamie and Anto steal a pile of questionnaires from the corner shop, squeeze them into paper balls and attempt to throw them over the peace gate to strike passers-by on the other side. Patricia catches them red-handed and almost runs them down with her wheelchair.

'Here, yousens, stap that nigh or I'll take my fists to youse!' she shouts.

'Aye, dead on,' says Seamie

'Aye, whoopty doo!' adds Anto.

Similarly, one evening after a long day of door-to-door surveying, Roberta and Jean stumble upon Sam and Lee making questionnaires into paper planes.

'This is class!' says Lee excitedly. 'It's like that fuckin' *Dambusters* filum, so it is!'

Sam folds the surveys into the shape of airplanes, then Lee sets them alight and attempts to fly them over the peace gate to singe the unseen enemy on the other side. One burning questionnaire falls back and sets Lee's baseball cap on fire.

'Oh, fuck – it's burnin' me bap!' cries Lee.

Sam falls over with laughter as Lee panics. 'You're on fire the night, Lee!' he says laughing.

'Oh, fuck!' cries Lee in a high-pitched voice as he stamps out the fire on his headwear.

'Ha ha! You're screamin' like a wee hussy, ya big Beirut!' mocks Sam.

Once Lee pats out the fire, he has to use his asthma inhaler to steady his breathing while Sam continues to laugh hysterically. Roberta and Jean eventually recognise the comedy of the incident and join in the laughter, much to Lee's disgust. Sometimes Lee gets fed up with being laughed at. Sam is a good mate, but it's as if he knows that in spite of all his boasts, Lee has never won a fight and he's still a virgin – that's if the fumble up the entry with Kylie with the pierced nose from Cambrai Street doesn't count.

A few days later Jean and Roberta are standing in a doorway with one of the new Polish neighbours who is struggling with some of the English in the questionnaire and much of the history of the peace wall. Roberta is earnestly filling in the answers on the questionnaire, but Jean is distracted by the sound of Seamie arguing with a pretty teenage girl wearing pyjamas and pushing a pram, just on the other side of the pedestrian opening in the peace gate.

'No, you can't!' shouts the pretty girl.

'Why not?' asks Seamie gently.

'Fuck you away off, wee lad, I'm not even talkin' to you!'

'But—'

'Fuck off!'

The baby in the pram starts to cry as her mother storms off.

'Did you see that over at the peace gate, Roberta?' says Jean.

'I know,' says Roberta, 'them wee girls go out in their jammies all the time. There's no shame nowadays.'

'No, I mean that wee lad Seamie,' says Jean. 'You don't think he's the daddy?'

At this very moment Seamie notices the women noticing. He spits heavily through the opening in the peace gate, pulls up his hood and walks off with his head down.

On the final day of surveying Jean and Roberta smile and wave goodbye to Martha Johnston, or Moanin' Martha as they call her, when they leave her front door on completion of the final survey. (They deliberately kept Martha to the end as they knew it would be a challenging interaction.)

'Who's payin' for this?' asked Martha. 'I hope you and that church that lets in too many Taigs now are not taking funding away from the community.'

Following completion of Martha's detailed dictated responses rejecting the very idea of the survey and asserting the need for the peace gate to remain closed forever, the two women are exhausted but share a great sense of achievement.

'Yer woman would put years on ye, so she would,' says Jean.

Roberta carries a large clump of completed questionnaires under her arm, unaware as she hobbles along that she drops a few of the questionnaires on the pavement and leaves a trail of consultation behind her. They continue onward to the meeting room in the church where all the surviving surveys are piled up on the table waiting to be analysed.

'Oh, I can't wait!' cries Roberta excitedly. 'It'll be like countin' the votes for *The X Factor*!'

17

The analysis begins the next day, and the women create an assembly line of sorting, recording and adding. It takes a whole week to analyse the surveys, to check and double-check so no one can say it was all made-up.

'It must be accurate and statistically valid,' says Bridget.

'Wha?' says Roberta.

'It has to add up right,' explains Jean.

Roberta makes the tea, Jean sorts the surveys, Patricia does the sums, Bridget checks everything is accurate and Wee Jack Surgeoner licks the floor clean of tray-bake crumbs after regular refreshment breaks.

Once the results of the survey have been analysed, the findings then have to be verified by Big Stan and Wee Malachy, who question everything from the authenticity of individual questionnaires to the accuracy of the maths. But Bridget is ready for them and has an answer for everything, and in the end the two community leaders have no option but to accept that the consultation has produced a valid result. Bridget even persuades the leaders of LIG and RIG to let her use one of their laptops to type up the main findings to print for distribution.

Keen to share the results as soon as possible, the GOGO Girls invite the PSNI and a representative of the European Union Peace and Reconciliation Funds to meet with them at their next campaign meeting. The young community police officer arrives first.

'Hello, ladies,' he says pleasantly, 'so how can I help your wee group. We've no funding with all the cuts, you know.'

Jean thinks he looks much too young to be a policeman as Bridget pours him tea and Roberta offers him a slice of piping hot apple tart.

'So,' begins Jean, with a new-found air of no-nonsense authority, 'seventy-eight per cent of residents on both sides of the community say they want the gate open during the day.'

The police officer raises his eyebrows in pleasant surprise while Roberta holds a spoon with a large dollop of fresh cream in front of his face.

'Do ye want fresh cream on your apple tart, constable?' she enquires.

'Sixty-two per cent say they want the peace wall removed in the next ten years,' says Jean.

'Seventy-one per cent say the police could be doing a better job at stopping rioting on the interface,' adds Bridget.

At this exact moment the young police officer burns his tongue on the piping hot apple filling in his tart and chokes for a few minutes.

'Are you alright, love?' asks Bridget.

'Yes, I'll be fine,' he replies, his face reddening.

'God, I thought for a minute we were goin' to have to do the Himmler manoeuvre on him!' exclaims Roberta.

Minutes later the shocked police officer retreats from the meeting with every relevant statistic noted neatly in his police notebook. This is clearly a matter for the higher-ups.

'He was a lovely wee fella, wasn't he?' says Roberta.

'Aye, but what's he gonna do about it? That's the question,' says Jean.

'He near shit himself!' says Patricia.

A few minutes later the next visitor to arrive is a well-dressed, middle-aged Peace funding officer. She nervously parks her sky-blue Volkswagen Beetle outside, fearing a malicious scratch or a hijacking because that's what they do with nice cars in West Belfast.

'Will the car be okay?' she asks.

'Yes, love, it's not Syria, so it's nat,' says Patricia.

Bridget pours more tea while Roberta offers the somewhat reserved funding officer a large piece of the sweetest of pavlovas.

Before the women can begin to explain their campaign, the funding officer begins a well-practised speech in automatic pilot. 'The EU Peace and Reconciliation Funds could offer your group up to two thousand pounds for a good project and I am prepared to consider giving you that.' She flicks back her hair proudly. 'I have received a complaint from a local resident that this campaign is taking all the funding from the community, but I have checked the database and I don't see any duplication of services.'

'I bet that was bloody Moanin' Martha,' whispers Jean.

'All you have to do is fill in a Part A application,' continues the funding officer, 'and then if that is satisfactory on every level you can complete a Part B application with a detailed business plan and budget spreadsheet on the SEUPB website.'

'On the wha?' asks Roberta.

'I can set you up with the login details for the eSystem if you give me your email addresses, which I will, of course, hold securely under GDPR,' she continues.

'What's she holdin' under the GPO?' whispers Roberta.

The funding officer shakes her head dismissively.

Roberta may have grown up in a children's home and gone to a special school, but she is sensitive to superciliousness and will not be patronised by anyone.

'Listen, love, my blind budgie talks more sense than you!' she says.

Jean kicks Roberta under the table.

'Listen, love,' interrupts Patricia, 'the only login I'm interested in is the log in the fire in my livin' room.'

Wee Jack lets out an odorous fart that everyone pretends hasn't happened and Patricia yawns loudly as the funding officer continues unperturbed, although now holding a perfumed tissue beneath her well-powdered nose, as she repeats in detail the whole laborious funding-application process.

'Then the assessment panel will mark your application against the required peace-outcomes criteria – both the verticals and the horizontals, such as impact on the environment, and then as long as you have satisfactory governance arrangements in place ...'

'Sure, Northern Ireland hasn't even got a satisfactory government in place,' whispers Bridget to Jean.

Patricia looks the funding officer up and down, then leans over and whispers to Jean, 'Sure, she's nearly our age. Mutton dressed as lamb.'

Jean nods and winks.

'... and on satisfactory fulfilment of the required monitoring and evaluation systems, and written assurances that you are fully compliant with GDPR, safeguarding, health and safety and have sufficient levels of public liability insurance ...'

Roberta feigns an exaggerated yawn.

'... we will release the first twenty-five per cent on condition that you provide at least three original quotes for all purchases and submit to our rigorous auditing requirements to ensure you are not committing fraud, and that means we will only pay out monies on receipt of all original invoices,' she says, as she looks accusingly at the pavlova and finishes with a flourish, 'for *everything*!'

Jean looks around at the blank expressions on the faces of her friends and without needing to consult the rest of the group says, 'Thanks, love, but no thanks. We're pensioners, you see. Half of us will be dead by the time we do all that.'

18

The sky spits on Belfast as Jean and Roberta share an umbrella on their regular route to the peace gate. Wee Rover McCracken and Big Petra Dougan are copulating beside the peace wall while a magpie on top of the wall spies on them like a winged voyeur. The women retract the umbrella for a few seconds to squeeze through the pedestrian opening made famous by Patricia's wheelchair protest, and then extend the umbrella once again as they emerge on the Catholic street on the other side of the peace wall. It continues to rain on both sides of the peace wall. It's almost as if God treats Catholics and Protestants the same.

'Meetin' all them very important people is a waste of time,' complains Jean to Roberta. 'They just think we're a clatter of silly oul dolls who haven't a clue.'

'I know, Jean,' Roberta replies. 'I always thought them Peace and Recreation Funds was for till help us with peace and all.'

For the first time since the campaign began, Jean is feeling downhearted. All their weeks of hard work with the door-to-door survey seems to have got them nowhere.

'I sometimes think we're wasting our time, Roberta, love,' she says. 'Maybe my Derek was right. Maybe it *is* better to keep your head down in this bloody country.'

'Now don't be saying that, Jean. You're just havin' a bad day. Sure, at least your Derek tried,' says Roberta.

It was true. Apart from all the threats he had received for bricklaying for the wrong sort, Derek had been threatened by the IRA in the 1970s for cradling a dying British soldier in his arms. The teenage soldier was shot in the back while on patrol on the main road as Derek was returning home from work. Instinctively Derek ran to the boy's aid but it was obviously too late, so he simply held the dying soldier in his arms, stroked his forehead and imagined what the poor boy's father and mother would say to him at this moment.

'You're alright, son,' he said. 'You're gonna be alright. The ambulance is on its way and your mother and father too. You know how much they love you, don't you, son?'

'Fuck the Brits!' shouted the passenger of a passing car while the other men inside cheered and made obscene gestures out the window towards Derek and the dying boy.

'You were a hero the day,' Jean had said.

'Some hero,' replied Derek, 'the wee lad still died.'

Jean couldn't get the bloodstains off Derek's overalls for weeks no matter how hard she scrubbed. Eventually she gave up and cut the material into strips that she burnt in the living room fireplace. The RUC called at the house and warned Derek that his life was under threat and it would be safer to get away for a while. Jean was three months pregnant with Wee Heather when Derek went to live in England. She insisted she was staying in her own home until her baby was born and no terrorist was going to stop her. It was only when Bridget got assurances from some Provo she had delivered in the Royal that Derek was able to return. Of course, it was too late for Wee Heather and Wee Jean. The doctor said it was the stress that brought on the premature birth and it was best for Jean to have the hysterectomy. Derek blamed republicans for Wee Heather until his dying day.

'Why would anyone want to live in a United Ireland ruled by them heartless bastards,' he often said.

Roberta nudges Jean when she notices Seamie and Anto standing around the corner, smoking and joking as usual. Anto notices the two little women emerging through the pedestrian entrance on his side of the peace gate.

'Look, Seamie,' he says pointing, 'here comes Wee Jean and a specky Susan fuckin' Boyle.'

Seamie is not amused. 'Wise up, Anto, Wee Jean's alright, so she is. Her oul fella was a brickie, ya know, and that oul doll with her's a harmless oul crater.'

'She's a wee Prod!' protests Anto. 'And her grandson's a fuckin' Brit, ya know! He's a legitimate target.'

'Well, you'd need to be a good shot to hit that target because he's in fuckin' Afghanistan,' Seamie replies. Then unexpectedly Seamie pushes Anto out of the way roughly with a disgusted expression on his face and says, 'Why are you such a wanker, wee lad?'

Anto is devastated but determined not to show it.

'At least my ma's not a wino!' he barks.

Seamie shoots a violent glance at Anto who immediately knows he has crossed a line. He backs down, looks at the ground and kicks the peace wall with all the masculinity he can muster.

'What about ye, Wee Jean?' says Seamie.

'Och, I'm alright, love,' replies Jean, turning towards the two young people for the first time. 'What about you? Any work?'

'What do you think?' sniffs Seamie.

'Did I see you the other day with that nice lookin' wee girl pushin' a pram when I was doing our wee survey round the doors?' she asks.

'Aye, that's the wain and Ann Marie. Well, she was my girl but I fell out with her. She does my head in, Jean,' Seamie replies.

'Aye, she treats him like dirt,' says Anto.

Seamie stands back and looks Anto up and down as if he has just landed from another planet. 'What the fuck would you know about it, wee lad?' he asks.

Jean pats him on the arm. 'She looked like a nice wee girl to me, so she did.'

'Jean,' exclaims Seamie, 'she takes the pram to Tesco and does the shappin' in her fuckin' jammies, for God's sake!'

Jean is disappointed. 'Well, I saw the way you two looked at each other. And don't you forget, son, you are responsible for that wee chile,' she says.

Seamie sniffs, shrugs his shoulders and walks away, leaving Anto alone kicking the peace wall.

'His big brothers are in good jobs in America, ya know!' says Anto proudly. He continues to abuse the peace wall until he kicks it too hard and hurts his foot but pretends to be too tough to feel the pain. He's still reeling from upsetting his best mate. Nothing is more important to him than approval from Seamie, and his hero has just taken the side of an old Prod woman over him. Anto is confused. He's known Seamie all his life. Sometimes he just wants to spend the whole day, every day, just with Seamie. He's terrified this might mean he's gay. That's just about the worst thing he could be round here. He doesn't want to kiss Seamie but sometimes he longs for his best mate to put his arm around him. He really needs to talk to someone about all this, but he knows if he shares these thoughts and feelings it would be the end of his world. Oblivious to Anto's inner struggles, Jean and Roberta shake their heads disapprovingly in the young man's direction and continue on their way to the latest GOGO Girls meeting in the church hall.

'He's a hateful wee skitter,' says Jean, 'but that Seamie's not such a bad wee lad, Roberta. He's just never had a chance.'

Roberta looks unconvinced. 'I'd trust him as far as I could throw him,' she replies.

19

The GOGO Girls seem to spend their whole lives criss-crossing the Belfast peace line. From Jean's house to the church hall, back and forwards they transgress these forbidden boundaries every day.

'We're to and fro here like a load of balls at Wimbledon,' jokes Patricia.

The women boldly go where few of their neighbours have gone before – except in an emergency, and for the GOGO Girls this cross-community life has become normal. It's almost as if the gate is open and the peace wall has been demolished already. The walls in their hearts disappeared years ago. Perhaps those invisible walls were never too high, even during the worst of times.

Today, as Jean and Roberta return from their latest meeting, they emerge from the pedestrian opening in the gate on the Protestant pavement to discover Sam and Lee kicking a football up against the gate outside Jean's house.

Roberta is immediately on the offensive. 'Have you wee lads nathin' better to do than keepy-yuppy outside Jean's house?'

'No, sure we're wee scumbegs, missus, remember?' replies Sam with a scowl.

Sam's problem is that he considers himself to be a bigger scumbag than anyone else, but he's not going to admit that to anyone round here. Lee is up for a confrontation. Last night his father got drunk at the drinking club he runs for Ulster and called Lee a 'fuckin' useless wee waste of space'.

'Aye, at least we're not Fenian lovers like yousens,' Lee says with a fulsome spit. 'You two spend more time on their side than our side.'

Jean steps in. 'For God's sake, will you forget about sides for once in your lives,' she says.

'Well, King Billy didn't beat the Taigs at the Battle of the Somme for nathin', ya know!' replies Lee.

Roberta looks wide-eyed at Lee. 'And youse all say I talk a lotta shite.'

Lee has not spent a great deal of time in education. He gets confused with words and compensates with bad behaviour and ultimately gets expelled from different schools before anyone has the time or interest to diagnose his dyslexia. On top of that, Lee's relationship with his father is strained. He is a big disappointment. Lee knows all the right words to be a paramilitary leader, but he lacks the physical bulk and inherent cruelty required to follow in his father's footsteps. For several years now he has lived with his much-older sister, Lynn – his mother always describes Lee as 'a wee late one'. Lynn has done her best for her brother but she has three children of her own to look after now, and it's been very hard since her husband ran off with the woman at the vape shop on the Eleventh Night. Lee's nightmares and asthma have been a constant worry for Lynn, but sometimes his mood swings are too much to bear and she loses her temper and tells him to move out and find a flat of his own and give her head peace.

Jean has no idea about the turmoil in Lee's life but today she is determined to get beyond all the usual banter and insults. She believes if she is kind to Sam and Lee, the teenagers might respond.

'Sam, when you did the boxin' with your daddy, it didn't matter what foot you kicked with,' she points out.

'Aye, or what hand you punched with,' adds Roberta.

Some of the boxing clubs in Belfast are renowned for being open to people from both sides. It's considered okay to enjoy boxing the jaws of both Protestants and Catholics.

Jean continues, 'Why don't you go back and help your daddy with his wee boxin' club? He's a great fella, you know.'

'Sure, you could be the next Farl Crampton,' says Roberta.

Sam responds swiftly, 'My da's more interested in boxin' and Jesus than he is in his own son.'

'Aye, his oul lad spends more time gettin' the whole street saved than takin' our Sammy to see a Rangers match like all the other das,' adds Lee.

'Keep you out of it!' snaps Sam. 'When was the last time your da took you anywhere? Was it Disney on fuckin' Ice?'

'Sam's father is a beautiful preacher of the Gospel,' says Roberta. 'I put my hand up to get saved at the end of one of his wee meetin's in the gospel hall, so I did.'

'Ach, Roberta, love, you put your hand up at the end of every wee meetin' you ever go to. You keep gettin' born again, again and again,' says Jean, and Sam rolls his eyes knowingly.

'Don't you be disrespectable to God, Jean Beattie,' warns Roberta. 'Remember John 6:13, "God so loved the world", so He did.'

Jean does not reply to Roberta as she is still taken aback by the bitterness in Sam's voice.

'Son, don't you be sayin' those awful things about your own flesh and blood. I remember when you were born – you were your daddy's wee pride and joy,' she says.

Sam looks down and under his breath says, 'I wish I never was fuckin' born.'

Jean is shocked. 'Sam, love, I heard that,' she says. 'Don't you be even thinkin' like that – ever! Do you hear me, wee fella?'

Jean is unaware of just how disappointed Sam's father was when his only son didn't follow in his footsteps and win the Belfast Junior League Boxing Cup. When Sam started to skip Sunday school and was caught smoking outside church one Sunday morning he brought shame upon the family. Jean has no idea what it felt like to be on the receiving end of a father's angry rebukes and the cold, disappointed silences. Her father, Geordie, was loved by everybody. He was known as a great character on the Road, with a mischievous sense of humour and a loyal band of friends. Jean's father had been nothing but warm, loving and accepting no matter what Jean chose to do in life.

Sam pulls up his hood, hangs his head and kicks the peace wall. Jean and Roberta realise the conversation is over. They link arms and walk across the road towards Jean's house. As she turns the key in her front door, Jean turns around and looks back at Sam with great concern.

Sam wanders off with familiar thoughts bubbling up in his head – what's the point of all this anyway? There's no future for me in this shithole. Would it matter if I just didn't wake up the marra? Sure, no one would give a fuck! These are the thoughts Sam shares with no one. Maybe I should talk to Wee Jean about all this? he thinks, but then changes his mind. Wise up, wee lad. You're only wasting your time here.

20

The next day Jean is deep in thought when Roberta calls to the house with a Tupperware box of apple creams from the car boot sale. Jean pours the tea while Roberta chatters about last night's TV.

'I love that *Casualty*, so I do,' she enthuses, 'especially all them lovely big English doctors. They can take my pulse any time, so they can. Sure, did you see yer man with the lovely teeth and the white coat and the stetherscope and all savin' yer woman that was in *Midsomer Murders* when she fell down the stairs by puttin' the jump leads till her ticker, even though he just found out his girlfriend's doin' a line with one of them other doctors on the sly, the wee hussy—'

The doorbell rings and Moanin' Martha is on the doorstep. Here we go, thinks Jean.

'Well, Jean, I'm just here to let you know that the community is not a bit happy with the Roman Catholics takin' over the Methodist church and applyin' to take all the funding away from the community ...'

Jean does not even attempt to interrupt or correct. She has heard all this before and knows nothing will convince Martha that the gate could ever be opened.

'So I just want to let you know that no matter what your wee survey said, the people and the organisations on this side will not allow that gate to be opened until ... until the other side apologises for thirty years of IRA terrorism!'

'Thanks for lettin' us know again, Martha,' says Jean at the end of the doorstep tirade. 'How's your Billy's ears anyway?'

'No better, Jean,' replies Martha more softly. 'He says he can hardly hear a word I say nigh. The only relief the poor crater gets is on the wee loop system in the pub. He has to go round there every night now.'

Jean nods knowingly and says a polite goodbye to Martha – until the next complaint.

'Sorry, I hid in your good room, love,' says Roberta when Jean returns to the kitchen. 'Yer woman would put years on you.'

Jean, not listening, begins and then suddenly stops pouring the tea and emerges from her thoughts. 'Right, that's it, Roberta,' she says. 'I know what I'm goin' till do.'

'Are you gonna watch *Casualty*?' asks Roberta.

'No, Roberta, will you listen for once in your life? You know that three thousand pounds Big Isobel left me to do up my workin' kitchen?'

'Yes, Jean, love. That was awful good of her.'

'Well, I've just decided what I'm gonna do with it,' says Jean.

Roberta looks at her old friend for a long time. Then she smiles. 'Och, Jean, you're not – are you?' she says.

Jean nods. It is a quiet and assured nod.

'You're goin' to see Cliff Richard in London, aren't you, Jean?'

'No, Roberta! Stop acting the lig. You know rightly what I'm going to do with the money.'

Roberta was not entirely sure but she was certain it would be something good. 'I just love you, Jean Beattie, so I do,' says Roberta hugging Jean, who wipes a tear from the corner of her eye.

This is what Roberta loves so much about Jean. She was like one of the kind older ladies she remembered from the children's home. Not like the grumpy men who shouted too much at her for not clearing up properly after playing with her dolls and blamed her for flooding the bathroom when she forgot to turn the taps off because a game of hide-and-seek had started.

'Away you go,' says Jean. 'You're missin' *Casualty*. I'll tell the girls at the meetin' the marra mornin'.'

21

'Melt ye!' says Jean.

'I know, I'm sweltered, so I am,' replies Roberta.

It's unusually bright and sunny the next morning when Jean and Roberta once again pass through the opening in the peace gate.

'We're in and out of this here gate like the dusty bluebells,' says Jean.

With temperatures in Belfast soaring, Roberta is holding an old pink portable battery-operated fan.

'This is like a million hot flushes all over again,' says Jean.

'Aye, nightmare! Tell me about it,' says Roberta.

Hot weather is rare in Belfast and is initially celebrated with cries of 'taps aff!', doorstep sunbathing and a disturbing level of exposed milky-white flesh. This is swiftly followed by a sharp spike in sales of fans, barbecues and aftersun lotion. After three consecutive days of Mediterranean climate the traditional pattern is that the joy of sunshine is replaced by fulsome sweaty moaning.

'I'm bloody baked, so I am,' complains Jean.

Unfortunately Roberta's ten-year-old fan has not been required for the past twelve months and it cuts out every few seconds until she bangs it with her fist. 'I blame that oul rip Trump,' she says. 'Sure, he doesn't even believe in climax change.'

Jean is purposefully carrying a biscuit tin containing her cash from Big Isobel's legacy as if it holds the Crown Jewels. 'You know what, Roberta, love?' she says. 'I slept like a wee baby last night, even with this oul heat and all. I'd none of my oul angina nor nathin'. That just shows I've made the right decision about Big Isobel's money.'

'I dreamt about that big English doctor in *Casualty*,' replies Roberta.

'Not a nightmare then, love?' says Jean.

Roberta has no idea what Jean is talking about and continues, 'And I was on a stretcher in the Royal and he came runnin' down the corridor and the next thing I knew he was pushing my chest up and down and up and down and … for God's sake, this wee fan is bloody useless, I'm sweatin' like a pig, Jean—'

'Roberta, love,' interrupts Jean, 'how many times do I need to tell you, you don't need a man to make you happy. Sure, haven't you survived this long without one?'

'Someday my prince will come, so he will,' says Roberta.

'Well, he's takin' his time,' says Jean.

'Och, Jean, I wish I'd had a wee Derek, like you did.'

'Och, sure an oul lad wouldn't do your blood pressure much good, Roberta, love,' says Jean.

Jean and Derek had married when she was eighteen years old. Derek had been her first boyfriend. Of course there had plenty of offers of a dance or two at the Ritz and the Floral Hall dances every Saturday night, but from the moment Jean noticed Derek doing the Hucklebuck she only had eyes for the wee bricklayer with the brown eyes from Berlin Street.

As they turn the corner on the way to their latest GOGO Girls meeting in the church hall, Jean notices a commotion on the street and stops dead. The two friends stand in shocked silence. Suddenly the siren of a fast-approaching fire engine breaks their stillness.

Jean stands frozen on the spot and looks towards the Methodist church. 'Oh. My. God!' she cries.

The church is on fire. Smoke is billowing through a window and is spiralling up the steeple. A magpie is squawking from the peace wall next door. Roberta grips Jean's arm tightly and starts to cry childlike tears.

'Oh, Jean, what have they done?' cries Roberta. Then she starts to scream, 'Oh, my God, oh, my God, oh, my God!'

Jean embraces Roberta like a mother with a hysterical toddler as a fire engine and police car pull up outside the church simultaneously with a startling wail of sirens and screeching of brakes. A team of firefighters and police officers leap from their vehicles with the firefighters swiftly unravelling the fire hoses and dowsing the flames coming from the window of the pensioners' meeting room. Dark smoke is billowing out the smashed window a petrol bomb was earlier thrown through.

Bridget and Patricia are already waiting at the police line in front of the church hall. They are clinging to one another, shaking.

'This is terrible – it's worse than Primark!' says Patricia.

Wee Jack is hiding, cowering and shivering under the shelter of Maureen O'Boyle's hydrangea bush in her tiny front garden on the other side of the road.

'It's like the Nottingham Cathedral in Paris all over again!' cries Roberta.

Jean clutches the biscuit tin close to her chest.

On the front wall of the church there is freshly daubed graffiti in white paint: *KILL THE COFFIN DODGERS.*

Wee Malachy arrives on the scene and approaches the women immediately. 'I just want to let you know that my community did nat sanction this action,' he says.

Bridget and Patricia nod and smile weakly.

Jean and Roberta shuffle forwards and stand in front of the graffiti, trembling, shoulder to shoulder and arm to arm in solidarity with Bridget and Patricia. A small crowd of local youths gather.

'Class!' shouts Anto at the sight of the flames.

'Ah, for fuck sake,' says Seamie.

Big Stan's black taxi arrives on the scene and he gets out to observe the damage. 'An unprovoked sectarian attack on a Protestant church by republican terrorists!' he announces.

Wee Malachy is clearly unimpressed by this accusation and sends one of his bodyguards over to speak to Stan's driver to demand an immediate retraction or a mediated dialogue.

'Clearly my community will not stay silent in the face of such unfounded accusations,' shouts Wee Malachy.

'Sure, when has he ever stayed silent about anything?' says Patricia.

The relationship between LIG and RIG is under stress and it is quickly agreed that all cross-community contact should be suspended until further notice, and emergency funding should be demanded from the council to facilitate talks between the two groups in a neutral venue, such as the Slieve Donard Hotel. As these street negotiations are taking place the smell and smoke of the burning sanctuary becomes overwhelming.

Observing the interactions between Big Stan and Wee Malachy, Bridget says, 'Those two skitters are goin' to make money out of this, just you see.'

The police ask the crowd to disperse for their own safety.

'I'm scared!' cries Roberta.

When the commotion dies down and the flames have been doused, the GOGO Girls retreat round the corner to Jean's house. They sit at Jean's kitchen table drinking copious cups of milky tea sweetened with bites of Scottish shortbread in an attempt to recover from the shock of the church attack. Jean has banned Wee Jack from her working kitchen for peeing up her purple pouffe, so he is yelping towards the clouds of smoke above Jean's backyard where he has been banished.

Jean is full of nervous energy and is refilling the teacups quicker than the women are drinking it. 'Who wants another wee warm?' she says.

Patricia is bursting with indignation. 'I'm tellin' ya, Jean,' she says, 'if I had my legs and I got my hands on the wee bastards that done this, they'd know all about bein' a coffin dodger!'

'I'm scared, Jean,' says Roberta, 'but we can't give up now, can we?'

The question sounds like a request.

'Can we, Jean?' repeats Roberta.

The women look around at one another in silence as if to enquire whether it's time to bring this dangerous folly to an end.

Bridget looks her age today. 'Calm down, girls,' she says sagely. 'There's no point in upsetting ourselves any more – sure, that's what they want, isn't it?'

Another thoughtful silence ensues for several minutes until Patricia's mobile rings. She looks at the number and smiles proudly. 'Now, guess who's phonin' *me* ... shh!' Proudly Patricia removes a large pink globe earring from her ear for the important phone call. 'Hello, Stephen ... yes ... yes, it's terrible, so it is, but I'm tellin' you here and now, and I'm tellin' you for nathin', we will not be intimidated by no one. Cowardly wee bastards threw a petrol bomb at a church and ran away. Threatened us and called us coffin dodgers, so they did ... I know, Stephen, it's a blinkin' disgrace. And how are you, love, anyhow? I hope you're keeping off them prawn cocktail crisps, and how's your mammy, love? ... And what's that? ... Yes, of course, yes, love, the GOGO Girls Campaign is definitely still on ... yes, love, I'll talk to you about it in the morning on the biggest show in the country ...'

The other women are clearly bemused by Patricia's intimate relationship with the famous BBC radio presenter. But suddenly the rapport is broken.

'What? Whad'ya mean an exclusive? And nat talk till no one else before I talk to you?' asks Patricia, with a sudden loss of warmth in her voice. 'No, sorry, Stephen, love, you're an awful nice fella and all but I'm very sorry, love, I'll talk to that lovely big Paul Clark on the UTV first and even that nice wee Welsh girl on *The One Show* if I want till, and no one, not even you, is gonna stop me!' and she hangs up and fixes her hair.

'Patricia, we haven't even talked to each other yet about what we're going to do and you're already away talking to half the friggin' journalists in Ulster!' says Jean.

'Are you losin' the run of yourself?' says Bridget.

Patricia looks offended.

'She'll be ringin' David Dumbledore at the BBC in London next,' says Roberta.

'Well, if you don't want me to be a GOGO Girl no more that's okay with me,' says Patricia.

'Nobody said that, Patricia,' says Jean.

'Aye, but that's what you meant, and my Wee Jack banned from the meetin's and all,' says Patricia. 'Maybe certain people are jealous of my media relationships.'

'Patricia, you don't have any media relationships – they're just using you,' says Bridget.

'Don't you dare talk to me like that, Bridget!' barks Patricia, and she storms out leaving Wee Jack behind in Jean's backyard.

'Jean's right,' says Bridget to the remaining group, 'we need to stand back and think about this. The more we say we want the gate open, the more we're being attacked by cowards in the shadows. And the question has to be asked – is it worth it? Will this place ever change?'

As Wee Jack begins to howl towards the billows of smoke outside, Jean quietly places the biscuit tin of money securely back in the cupboard.

'Let's sleep on it, girls,' she says. 'I'm not one for giving up but this is gettin' serious.'

22

'Jean?'

'Yes, Patricia, love?'

'I was just calling to ask you if we're still meetin' today?' asks Patricia in her sheepish little-girl voice.

'Well, now we've nowhere to meet,' says Jean.

Patricia regrets storming out the day before. She had to ask Bridget to retrieve Wee Jack. Today she has decided to continue as if the argument never happened. She knows that good friends can forgive and forget very quickly.

'I know, Jean, love, but that lovely big educated fella from the Good Community Relations Conference is just off the phone with me and he says he's still comin' up to see us this afternoon with them women from Rwanda he told us about, and they want to support the GOGO Girls because of the petrol bomb attack on the church and all. I haven't phoned Nolan yet because I wanted to tell you first, Jean.'

'Oh, my God, Patricia, with all the upset I forgot about that,' says Jean.

'What are we goin' to do?' asks Patricia.

'Well, first of all, you're not going anywhere near any bloody journalists, Patricia. Okay, let me think—'

'What if Sir Trevor McDonald phones me?'

'Patricia – catch yerself on!'

'Sorry, Jean, I don't know what to do. I haven't slept a wink thinkin' about that friggin' fire at our wee meetin' room and that petrol bomb, and the smoke reminded me of that day at the post office, and, oh, my God, Jean, it was terrible that day.' Patricia begins to cry.

'Och, shush now, Patricia, love,' says Jean. 'You calm yerself. Ask Liam to make you a nice cup-a-tay—'

'But he's at the bookies.'

Jean rolls her eyes. 'Well, make yourself a nice cup-a-tay, love, and sit down and calm yourself. It'll be alright. I promise you.'

'Okay,' says Patricia, starting to calm down a little, 'but I'm already sittin' down in case you'd forgotten.'

'Now, if those poor women from Rwanda can survive what they went through, then I think the women of West Belfast can get over yet another bloody petrol bomb,' says Jean, more resolute. 'Phone yer man with the bicycle clips and tell him we'll meet them at the peace wall in Lanark Way and youse can all come back to my house after, and I'll let Bridget and Roberta know the plans. Okay?'

'Okay. Thanks, Jean, love,' says Patricia, and the two women hang up their phones to prepare to meet the visitors from Rwanda.

Jean gets to work cleaning up the kitchen and prepares a pavlova even though she's not sure if Rwandans eat pavlova.

A few hours later the GOGO Girls are waiting beside the huge iconic peace wall that has divided neighbours on the Falls and Shankill Roads for over fifty years. The British army installations and the ring of steel around the city centre are distant memories, but this massive structure remains unbowed by an end to violence, a peace process and power-sharing between Unionists and Nationalists. It's almost as if someone somewhere still benefits from keeping the people of Belfast apart. There is very little trouble round here nowadays – the biggest danger is being trampled on by a coachload of tourists. They come from all over the world and disembark from their buses to be horrified at how divided Belfast remains to this day, before writing a John Lennon lyric on the peace wall. Scores of black-taxi tours come and go with earnest tourists trying to understand why Catholics and Protestants in Ireland are still separated by walls in the twenty-first century when there's been peace for twenty years and they're all Christians anyway. The black-taxi tour guides generally tell them it was all the Brit's fault and thank them for their tips and support for a United Ireland. As soon as the tourists have been horrified for a few minutes they are whisked away to spend their money in other parts of the city with the deep satisfaction that comes from knowing that by signing their name on the peace wall they have helped bring peace in Ireland.

'Look at the cut of thon over yonder,' says Patricia pointing to an American tourist wearing a red *Make America Great Again* baseball cap, shaking his head in solemn disbelief and signing the peace wall.

'Sure, themuns want a far bigger wall than this to stop all them poor wee Mexican caravanners invadin' America,' says Roberta.

Just then a regular taxi pulls up beside the GOGO Girls.

'Oh, look, they've come in a Wuber!' says Roberta.

The lovely big educated fella from the Good Community Relations Conference gets out of the taxi in his corduroys along with two middle-aged African women wearing brightly coloured traditional clothes and headscarves.

'Oh, youse twos are gorgeous,' says Patricia, shaking the women's hands warmly.

'Are you not on your bike for the environment today, love,' says Jean to the lovely big educated fella.

'You've still got your bicycle clips on,' points out Roberta.

'Absolutely!' he replies. 'This is Grace and Alice from Rwanda. Grace speaks very good English.'

'Pleased to meet you,' says Bridget, almost bowing to the two smiling visitors. 'I'm Bridget, and this is Jean, and Roberta and this is Patricia in the wheelchair.'

'You have suffered much,' says Grace to Patricia as she shakes her hand.

'Och, don't you worry about me, love,' Patricia says. 'You're very welcome to West Belfast.'

'Thank you,' says Grace. 'This morning we visited Stormont to meet your brave politicians who made the peace.'

'Never worry about them, love. What do you think of our wonderful peace wall?' says Jean.

Grace and Alice walk along the pavement beside the peace wall, scanning its great height and huge length.

'This is how you live?' asks Grace, before turning to Alice and speaking in an African language for a few minutes.

The visitors shake their heads.

'It's not the way we want to live but nobody up at Stormount is listening to us,' says Bridget.

'I'm sorry, my friend,' says Grace, 'but if this is how you live, your peace process is worthless. Your politicians have failed.'

'That's exactly what I think,' says Jean, pleasantly surprised by the candid perspective of a fresh pair of eyes from Rwanda.

'When the human heart turns to evil, no wall is tall enough or long enough to protect you,' says Grace. 'Your wall cannot protect you from hatred.'

As the women walk along the peace wall, Grace tells her story of how she and millions of Tutsis were attacked by machete-wielding killing gangs for days on end, how she hid in the mud of the swamps and the forests and ultimately escaped when many she knew and loved, including her mother and sister, died in the genocide. The Belfast women listen in complete silence.

'The dying whispered in the mud but no one heard their last words and no one came to their aid,' says Grace.

'Thank God that didn't happen here,' says Jean. 'We thought it was bad here but we've no idea. How did you get on with your lives again after all those terrible things were done to you?'

Grace continues to walk slowly along the perimeter of the peace wall. 'I ran away from the evil and I thank God I survived,' says Grace. 'We were supposed to be wiped from this earth but I am still here. I looked after four children who were left without a father or mother. I had already raised my own three children, but these little ones were orphans and I am a mother and so I did what I knew best how to do.'

Jean, Bridget, Patricia and Roberta are quietly weeping as they listen intently to every word Grace speaks. They take her and Alice's hands and continue along the wall. The Belfast women feel a solidarity with these two strangers from East Africa.

'People here don't want to forget or forgive each other,' says Jean. 'That's why this wall is still here.'

'It is very hard to forgive,' says Grace sadly. 'Today in my community the survivors and the killers share the same hilltops again. Fifteen years ago they released my mother's killer. He returned to be my neighbour in the next farm. There is no wall to keep us apart. I see him every day and I must choose to hate or to forgive. It is very hard, my friends. How can I reconcile evil and forgiveness?'

'Well, if people in Rwanda can manage to live again as neighbours after genocide, why can we not live without a wall between us in Belfast?' asks Bridget.

'Absolutely!' says the lovely big educated fella who has been following close behind.

Alice explains something to Grace that she wants her to share with the Belfast women.

'Some of the men who killed Alice's husband have baked bricks for her farm. Some of those men have fallen into despair but others are able to find some peace of mind by asking for forgiveness and trying to make amends, even though they feel it is undeserved.'

Jean embraces Alice. 'You're an amazing wee woman,' she says.

Alice smiles broadly with tears in her eyes.

'We can learn a lot from you,' says Bridget. 'You've heard about our wee campaign to get our gate open and the threats and attacks that have come our way. What do you think we should do?'

Alice talks to Grace in her own language for a few minutes.

'Alice says you will never have true peace in this city while the walls in your hearts and the walls on your streets remain.'

'This is unbelievable,' says Patricia. 'I've spent my whole life thinkin' we had to help all them poor wee Africans, and the first time I meet someone from there she helps me.'

'Absolutely!' says the lovely big educated fella.

Grace stops under the shadow of the peace wall and turns to speak directly to the four women. 'Courage takes me by the hand every day and despite all the pain life still offers me smiles,' she says.

Alice takes from her pocket four beautiful beaded African bracelets and gives them to Jean and the others.

'These are for you,' says Grace. 'These bracelets are made by the daughters of survivors and the daughters of the killers, together. After the killing is over, we can make beautiful new things with each other.'

'Thank you, love. God bless you,' says Jean, once again moved to tears by the women's generosity and support.

The women continue along Lanark Way in silence until they reach the gate. Jean invites the visitors in for a cup of tea and apologises to the lovely big educated fella for not having vegan tray bakes. The women talk for several hours about their families and food and traditions in their countries, long past the allotted time. Grace and Alice enjoy their first taste of pavlova, although they can't help laughing at the miniature-sized fruit on top. After a while Alice shares through Grace more of the horror of the genocide and her experience of hope and forgiveness and reconciliation. The GOGO Girls are aghast at the evil that was unleashed in Rwanda and the reconciliation journey many survivors have taken.

'Alice is a saint!' says Jean.

'She's not a saint, she's just a good woman like you, my sister, and there are many more like her in our villages in the hills,' says Grace.

The GOGO Girls have never heard the like of this in Belfast. No one talks much about forgiveness in this city – not in church, not in school and certainly not in Stormont. Perpetrators of violence hardly ever seek forgiveness and their victims seldom want to give it.

'We have peace but not much reconciliation here,' says Bridget.

'It seems your people want to live peacefully alongside each other but they do not want to live together with each other,' comments Grace.

'That's it,' says Jean. 'That's where we're at.'

When the Rwandan women depart it feels as if their visit has been too short.

'Girls, I don't know about you,' says Jean, 'but if the weemin in Rwanda can forgive killers in a genocide, I think we should be able to move on from some pathetic wee petrol bomber.'

'I agree,' says Bridget. 'I believe God sent us those two angels to show us the way.'

After the shock of the attack on the church, two women from a village in Rwanda leave the GOGO Girls with a sense of perspective, some healing following the trauma of recent days and a new determination to continue with the journey on which they have begun, no matter what trials may lie ahead.

'So we're not givin' up then?' asks Roberta.

'No bloody way!' announces Patricia.

This time there is no celebration and no singing. The four women put on their Rwandan bracelets and hold hands together around Jean's kitchen table. They close their eyes and Bridget says a prayer. Opening their eyes, they look around the little circle of friends and share a determined smile.

23

'So we're goin' to keep goin', arewen't we?' asks Roberta nervously, looking towards the ceiling of Jean's working kitchen.

'Well,' begins Patricia, 'my Liam says we should keep goin'. He says everyone in the bookies is right behind us.'

'I had a dream last night after we met the Rawandesian women,' says Roberta.

'Oh, please, not another dream about thon doctor in *Casualty*!' says Jean.

'No, Jean Beattie,' protests Roberta, 'there's more to me than just fancyin' a gorgeous big cardimologist on the TV, ya know.'

'Well, what then, Roberta?' asks Bridget.

'I dreamt it was the year 2025 and I was walkin' along our street and the cars were all space-age and silver and flyin', and I came to the gate and guess what? It was gone. And guess what? The whole peace wall had completely disappeared too. And you were there, Jean, and you took my hand and we skipped across to Bridget's street and Patricia was there and she jumped out of her wheelchair and did the Macarena with Wee Bertie who was still alive. And Alice and Grace from Rwanda showed up and started singin' lovely African songs, and the lovely big educated fella from the Good Community Relations Conference was dancing around in a grass skirt with coconut diddies like the bear in *The Jungle Book*—'

'Dear God,' says Jean.

'And everybody was happy and all the wee childer from both sides were playin' in the same streets together and were holdin' hands and goin' to the same schools together and playin' the same sports together, and the sun was shinin' and Geordie Best arrived and presented the GOGO Girls with a World Cup for gettin' our gate open, and Big Stan and Wee Malachy had got married – seriously, the DUP even let them! And Daniel O'Donnell arrived in a black taxi and started singin' "Over the Rainbow" and I was wearing red slippers like Dorothy and it was all amazin', so it was!'

The other women look at Roberta in stunned silence as they attempt to visualise the dream she has just described.

'So are we gonna keep goin'?' asks Roberta.

Finally Jean speaks up. 'Of course we're gonna keep goin',' she says. 'If nothing else, the petrol bomb decided it for me. No wee hood with a petrol bomb is gonna stop us now. They've ruled round here long enough. When are we finally goin' to stand up to all them bullies?'

'I'm not for giving up either,' agrees Bridget, 'not after what I heard about what those women in Rwanda have been through. But now we have nowhere to meet as well as no money.'

Roberta casts a glance towards Jean.

'Well, I wanted to talk to youse all about that anyway,' says Jean lifting her biscuit tin from the sideboard.

'Oh, my God!' gasps Roberta. 'Jean, you're not still gonna –'

'Big Isobel, God love her,' begins Jean, 'left me this here money to do up my working kitchen.' Jean opens the biscuit tin to reveal three hundred ten-pound notes to the sound of gasps from the other women. 'I won't need the half of it,' Jean explains, 'if I get some of them wee lads, like Sam and Seamie, with no jobs to do all the work—'

'Och, that's awful good of you, Jean,' interrupts Patricia. 'That wee lad Seamie's mother drinks every penny that ever comes into that house, you know. When his da left she went to bits and that wee lad never had a chance—'

'His brothers got away to America but that wee lad got into trouble with the police and they won't let him in over there now,' explains Bridget.

'Why would anyone want to get in there with that skitter Trump in charge?' interrupts Patricia. 'Sure, he wants a big wall even bigger and longer than our peace wall to keep all the Muslims in Mexico out of Dallas—'

Now it is Roberta's turn to interrupt. 'Patricia, houl your horses for a wee minute till you hear this.'

'So,' Jean continues, 'I'm givin' the other fifteen hundred pounds to the Get Our Gate Open Campaign.'

Bridget and Patricia stare at Jean with a mix of disbelief and pride. Roberta nods towards her friends knowingly, puffed up with pride that she was the first one to know about this important news.

'Jesus, Mary and Joseph, Jean, you're a saint!' cries Bridget with a single clap of her hands beneath her chin. Then she stands up and kisses Jean on the cheek.

'You may be four foot nathin', Jean, but you have the biggest heart in Belfast!' says Patricia, wiping tears from her eyes.

Jean blushes and continues with a no-nonsense announcement, 'And we can meet in here from now on.'

'And wait till youse hear what she wants to spend the money on,' adds Roberta with another knowing grin.

Jean stands up and announces, 'The GOGO Girls are goin' to get the gate opened for one whole day … for a … street party!'

'Like the Royal Jubilee,' says Roberta.

'Except cross community,' says Jean. 'For everybody!'

'But the peelers will never let the gate be opened,' frets Patricia.

'We can show them the results of our wee survey again,' suggests Bridget. 'It says seventy-eight per cent of people round here want the gate opened during the day.'

Jean nods. 'The PSNI will have some explainin' to do if they take the side of the ones who *never* want the gate opened,' she says.

'Like Moanin' Martha,' says Roberta, rolling her eyes.

'Oh, right nuff!' chuckles Patricia. 'If they refuse to open the gate, I'll tell Nolan.'

'I'm still scared,' says Roberta. 'What if them wee hoods go on their computers and get all their mates on TubeFace to attack us again?'

'They wouldn't have the guts to do that at a street party in broad daylight,' reasons Bridget.

'Them cowards creep around in the dark when people can't see their faces,' says Jean.

'And maybe they're not so young, the one's doing this, after all,' says Bridget.

The other women nod thoughtfully at Bridget's remark. Once again they fall silent for a moment.

'We'll do it for Big Isobel!' proclaims Jean.

'We'll do it for all the weemin round here who never get listened till!' says Patricia.

'We'll do it for our grandchildren!' says Bridget.

'Okay, we'll do it for *all* the wee childer round here!' says Roberta.

'We'll do it for ourselves,' says Jean quietly.

Patricia is moved and inspired and drives her wheelchair forwards to the top of the kitchen table. She looks around at the GOGO Girls and begins to sing earnestly but slightly out of tune. 'There's something inside so strong, so there is. I know that I can make it cos themuns are doing me wrong so wrong ... so they are ...'

The other women look on with a mixture of affection and embarrassment as Patricia sings her protest song and forgets the rest of the words.

'There's something inside dead strong, so there is, da da da da ... something inside dead strong.'

In the street outside Wee Jack hears the protest song and begins to howl an accompaniment on Jean's bleached front step. The noise frightens the magpie away, but not before he drops a light teardrop of white shit on the top of the peace gate.

24

With renewed resolve the women waste no time in turning Jean's street-party dream into a reality. The first step is a meeting in the local police station between Jean and Bridget and the district PSNI to seek permission for the public event.

'Now, sergeant, you let themuns have their parades and themuns have their protests, so I don't see why you wouldn't let a clatter of harmless oul dolls have a street party,' says Jean firmly.

'Well, of course, our priority is public safety,' advises the sergeant.

'But, sergeant,' asserts Bridget, 'the longer you keep these walls up the longer you provide a place for youngsters to go and throw stones at their neighbours when they're bored, and it's your officers who have to deal with it.'

'I know,' replied the sergeant in agreement. 'These days the peace walls are magnets for the sort of trouble they were put up to stop.'

'Well, then,' says Jean, 'you'll support our application to get the gate open for the day?'

'But we need to consult with all the key stakeholders before making a decision,' continues the police officer, as if reading from a script.

'You mean you need to ask Big Stan and Wee Malachy for their permission!' retorts Jean.

'But, ladies,' says the officer, shaking his head, 'local community representatives speak on behalf of their communities and the local elected representatives need to be—'

'Well, here, sergeant,' interrupts Jean, 'is this not representative enough for ye?'

The women produce a pile of hundreds of surveys from the confines of their shopping trolleys and load up the sergeant's desk with clear evidence that the majority of local residents on both sides of the peace wall want to see the peace gate open during the day. The sergeant examines the paperwork carefully and looks genuinely impressed.

'Okay, I'll do what I can, but there's a lot of documentation and health and safety and insurance to think about, you know, dear,' he says.

'We'll do whatever it takes,' says Jean firmly.

The women are undeterred and within a few weeks permission is granted and the date for the GOGO Street Party is set. Patricia, with her prominent media profile on *The Nolan Show* and renown as the woman stuck in the gate on the front page of the *Belfast Telegraph*, offers to phone the offices of the local MLAs to ask for their support. The Northern Ireland government has a goal for the removal of all the peace walls by 2023, but progress is painfully slow. So slow it seems it may not be a priority at all.

'You know the way yousens up at Stormount are paid to make this a better place,' she says,' and you know the way youse are awful busy up there not bein' our government, and havin' more of your talks about not wantin' to give in to the other side and all? And you know the way youse have said you want the peace walls to come down but not until the local residents want it, and then youse never do nathin' about it because it'll nat get youse no votes ...'

The hapless MLAs dare not interrupt.

'Well, the weemin residents of West Belfast are savin' youse a lotta time by startin' a campaign to take down the peace walls, and you can come to our street party the day we get the gate open to show everyone round here that that's what you want too ... You'd be made very welcome, so you would, and we'll give you a nice cup-a-tay and a tray bake – but if you don't show up, I'm reportin' you to Stephen Nolan!'

At the end of this series of awkward telephone conversations it remains unclear whether any of the elected Members of the Legislative Assembly will have time to squeeze the street party into their incredibly busy schedules.

Jean begins a marathon baking challenge. Her goal is to provide enough pavlovas to feed the whole street for a day. Gradually, as she whisks and bakes at speed, her kitchen table begins to fill up with a mountain range of pavlovas. The harder she works in her working kitchen the more she longs for the day her favourite room will be refurbished with the money from Big Isobel's legacy, but she has put this on hold for now for the sake of the campaign.

Patricia and Bridget are busy putting up posters for the street party on the Catholic side of the gate and are so focused on the task in hand that they ignore Seamie and Anto who are street drinking as usual.

Seamie is clearly drunk as he puts his arm round Anto. 'You're a good mate, Anto, even if you are a useless wee shite,' he says.

Anto could not be happier.

Patricia slaps on the glue with a paintbrush from Liam's shed and Bridget uses her height to affix the posters as high as possible on every available public space.

'I hope no one complains about us sticking these posters up everywhere, Patricia, dear,' frets Bridget.

'Well, here, Bridget, if we were puttin' up flegs or paintin' kerbstones, no one would dare question it, so God love anyone who comes up to me complainin' about a few wee posters for a street party!'

Wee Jack's tail wags more excitedly with every mounted poster, like a windscreen wiper in an Irish monsoon. Seamie and Anto look on in drunken disbelief at the extent of the pensioners' efforts.

'You know what, Anto?' says Seamie.

'Wha?' replies Anto.

'Them oul dolls would do your fuckin' head in but, you know, they lived through all that crap in the seventies, before we were even born, and they just want to make it better round here for all of us.'

'Don't be a fruit,' spits Anto. 'They're wastin' their time. Nobody cares if that wall never comes down.'

Seamie shakes his head and finishes his bottle of Buckfast.

Jean takes a break from baking to assist Roberta in gluing up posters for the street party on the lampposts on the Protestant side of the gate.

'When I was a wee girl I used to swing on them there lampposts,' says Roberta. 'It was great craic, so it was. I was like one of them wee blades in the Circular De Solielles until my rope got tangled and I banged my bap on the lamppost and fell off into dog's dirt.'

'That would explain a lot,' says Jean under her breath.

On this side of the peace line it's Sam and Lee who are looking on in disdain. While Jean and Roberta are sticking a poster to a nearby lamppost, Lee steals a pot of poster glue from under the women's noses and attempts to sniff it. Sam used to be partial to a good dose of glue-sniffing but on this occasion he declines to participate as he thinks you should grow out of glue-sniffing by the age of fourteen.

'What are you – a wee kid?' he asks Lee.

Lee is undeterred. However the glue is not strong enough to have the desired effect and instead of producing a hallucinatory high the adhesive sets off his allergies. Lee reaches for his asthma inhaler, attempting to recover both breath and a semblance of masculine composure.

'It's nat good pure stuff, that,' he sniffs, 'not like my wacky baccy.'

'What are you like, wee kid?' mocks Sam with a disgusted eye-roll.

Slowly but surely the pile of ten-pound notes in Jean's biscuit tin begins to diminish as she distributes money to the GOGO Girls to cover the mounting costs of the oncoming street party, and of course, Patricia becomes a regular attraction on the phone-in to *The Nolan Show* to update the public on the campaign and the street party.

'And here's Patricia from West Belfast again,' announces Stephen with a weary sigh.

'Hello, Stephen, love, how are you the day? Never you mind all themuns that says you're paid far too much and all you do is stir it up. The GOGO Girls are having a street party and we've got the PSNI to agree to open the gate for a whole day so that both sides can have a cross-community cheese and ham sandwich and a wee bun and a cup-a-tay ... And you're very welcome to come, Stephen, and I know you're watchin' your weight but you'd love Wee Jean's pavlova ... And everyone's welcome, so they are. There's even wee Polish neighbours and all comin', and we welcome everyone Stephen – Catholics, Protestants, Muslims, Jews and the LBQT community and everyone, and how's your mammy, love?'

Many callers to the radio programme are supportive of the street party. A taxi driver phones in to offer free transport for the elderly, and a student from the Holylands asks if he and his mates can come along if they bring their own sofa and some cider. A woman from the Lisburn Road offers to contribute some vegan canapés. However, predictably, a few callers are less supportive. Moanin' Martha herself calls in to inform the public that nobody asked the community's permission for the street party and she asks who is paying for it anyway, and then a regular caller from East Belfast complains that his community has been excluded once again by the West Belfast mafia. Only one or two members of the public call in to suggest Patricia should have her head examined.

As the day of the street party draws near, the interest in the GOGO Girls Campaign grows across Belfast. Patricia's phone is buzzing with requests for interviews from German radio stations and American PhD students. The front page of the *Belfast Telegraph* reads: More Women Across Belfast Join Campaign To Remove Peace Walls. Such is the public interest in the campaign that the women are invited to Belfast City Hall to discuss their demands with their local councillors.

25

The GOGO Girls arrive at the front of Belfast City Hall in a taxi.

'Isn't Uber class?' says Patricia, as the driver assists her back into her wheelchair. 'You just press a button on your mobile and a lovely big fella from Dunmurry or Africa comes and collects you at your front door.'

'No, that's Tinder, love!' says the taxi driver laughing.

No one gets the joke.

As he drives off, the four women look up towards the imposing dome of Belfast City Hall.

'I can't believe we've been invited here to meet the council,' says Jean.

'It shows they're starting to take us seriously,' says Bridget.

'We'll see,' says Patricia. 'They're all out for themselves in there, I'm tellin' ye.'

Roberta smiles as she admires the dome of the city hall. 'Just think of all the brilliant fights they've had in there over the years.'

Slowly the GOGO Girls make their way to the front door of the grand old building.

'The good and equal relations manager said she would meet us at the front door at half past,' explains Jean.

Inside, a friendly young woman with curly hair, scarlet acrylic nails and an iPad meets the women. 'Welcome to Belfast City Hall,' she says. 'Some of the councillors are waiting for you upstairs.'

'Your hair and your wee tablet's lovely,' says Roberta.

'Did you never want to give them nails a good bite?' asks Patricia.

As the good and equal relations manager leads them towards the lift, Jean spots a veteran of the council in the corridor.

'Look, girls!' she says, 'there's yer man from the UUP from the TV. I like that oul fella.'

'Sure as you're livin',' says Patricia, 'he's been a councillor since your granny was a girl.'

''Scuse me, councillor!' calls Roberta, stopping the elected representative in his tracks.

'We're the GOGO Girls from West Belfast and—'

'Oh, yes, I heard you on the radio. Tremendjus campaign!' says the councillor.

'We're here to ask the council to support the campaign to get our gate open so we can be good neighbours again,' says Bridget.

'You're very welcome to Belfast City Hall,' says the councillor. 'Just you talk to any of my staff here and they'll help you out. The council staff do a tremendjus job.'

'Yer man thinks everything's friggin' tremendjus,' whispers Patricia in Jean's ear.

'Can I just say it does my heart good to see a group of old dears like you coming together to do some good,' says the councillor.

The women decide it's time to move on.

'Hope you get a tremendjus vote the next time,' says Patricia dramatically as she swivels her wheelchair in the opposite direction and leads the women towards the lift.

The good and equal relations manager is still laughing when the lift arrives upstairs among the hallowed offices of the councillors.

'Where's the SDLP?' asks Bridget.

'I've no idea,' says the good and equal relations manager. 'There aren't as many SDLP here as there used to be, and a lot of councillors are in Newry today at a big conference on Brexit and the backstop.'

'Well, we want to have a word with all the parties before we leave this place today,' says Bridget.

'So everyone is away to make sure there's a soft border in Newry but we've still got a hard border between the Falls and the Shankill in West Belfast?' says Jean.

'I'd love to give them all a good kick up the backstop,' says Patricia.

'You'll meet the Sinn Féin councillor first, in here,' explains the good and equal relations manager gesturing to an office door, 'and then we'll go down the corridor to meet the DUP councillor.'

'Wha?' says Jean. 'Can they not meet us together?'

'We're cross community, why can't they be?' asks Patricia.

'The members prefer to do it this way on sensitive issues like this,' explains the good and equal relations manager with just a hint of an eye-roll.

'No wonder this country's in the state it's in!' says Patricia.

'Calm down, Patricia, we're goin' in to see the Shinners now, and you and I know they don't respond well to criticism,' says Bridget.

Patricia nods meekly as the good and equal relations manager leads them into the Sinn Féin councillor's office.

After a series of smiles and friendly handshakes Bridget presents the case for opening the gate, the findings of the community survey and plans for the forthcoming street party. (The women decided in advance that the Catholics should do most of the talking to Sinn Féin and the Protestants to the DUP, to increase their chances of being listened to.)

'Go raibh maith agat,' begins the councillor, 'clearly it's good to hear the voice of the local community and clearly we support equality for all.'

'That's brilliant,' says Patricia. 'So when are you goin' to get our gate open?'

'Well, clearly, as you know, the council does not have the powers to make this decision as responsibility for the interface barriers rests with Stormont and the NIO and, clearly, until there is a comprehensive agreement on all outstanding matters—'

'But will you come to the street party to support us then?' interrupts Patricia.

'As I'm sure the equality manager has explained, clearly there are a range of issues in the context of our peace strategy that need to be—'

'My Uncle Billy's doin' DJ at the street party, councillor,' interrupts Roberta. 'If you come and support us, I promise you I'll ask him to see if he can get "Agadoo" in Irish from the interweb and play it just for you.'

The Sinn Féin councillor continues with several minutes of policy speak on equality and rights and the legacy of the conflict due to the British presence in Ireland until finally he asks, 'Have you spoken to Malachy from the Republican Interface Group? The council fund him and he's doing a great job in breaking down barriers with the sectarian side of the community in West Belfast.'

'Friggin' RIG!' whispers Jean.

'Yes, we've spoken to Malachy on several occasions,' explains Bridget, 'but our campaign does not seem to be a big priority to him.'

'Well, clearly Malachy has been working on the ground for twenty years to reduce the social deprivation indices in the most disadvantaged communities in the six counties,' explains the councillor.

'And has it got any better?' asks Jean cheekily, unable to control herself.

'Clearly the years of structural and social injustices inflicted on West Belfast by successive British Tory governments are not going to go away overnight,' explains the councillor, clearly not for the first time.

'Sounds like Wee Malachy has a job for life,' says Jean.

The good and equal relations manager realises the tone of the conversation is beginning to deteriorate, and in an attempt to maintain good relations interjects that the councillor is very busy and the DUP councillor is waiting for them and he's a very busy man too.

Within minutes the GOGO Girls arrive in a parallel universe in the DUP councillor's office. Once again, after a friendly welcome and a few comments about the weather, the women present their case with Jean taking centre stage this time.

'Thank you, Jean,' says the DUP councillor. 'I've heard about the good work the church is doing up there on the peace line despite all the attacks from republicans.'

'So will you get our gate open then, councillor?' asks Jean.

'Unfortunately it's not up to me,' the councillor explains. 'You see, the council does not have responsibility for the peace walls – it's a Stormont matter, and until there is a comprehensive agreement on all outstanding matters—'

'But will you come to the street party to support us?' interrupts Jean.

'As I'm sure the good relations manager here has explained, you could perhaps apply for a small grant to help with the costs—'

'If you come to our street party, councillor, we promise there'll be no gay cakes. My Uncle Billy's doin' DJ and he does it at the Field on the Twelfth every year, councillor, and if you come and support us I'll make sure he doesn't play nathin' LGQT by the Village People or Elton John, except "Candle in the Wind", of course, but that was for Diana, God love her, she was the queen of the people's hearts, so she was.'

After an embarrassing pause, when the good and equal relations manager appears to stifle a laugh into her handkerchief, the DUP councillor explains that he has nothing against gay people as long as their abomination is not recognised in marriage.

'Don't forget we're the party of Christian morality,' he explains.

'Aye, yes, we know all about that, love, with the free heatin' and the free holidays and all,' interrupts Patricia.

After quoting several verses from the Bible the DUP councillor finally asks, 'Have you spoken to Big Stan from the Loyalist Interface Group? The council supports him and he's doing a great job in stopping republicans claiming all the funding in West Belfast.'

'Friggin' LIG!' whispers Jean. 'Yes, we asked Big Stan to support us but he says we don't represent his community because we're not paramilitaries,' she explains.

'We condemn all paramilitary activity on both sides,' says the councillor.

Once again, the good and equal relations manager recognises a need to bring the conversation to a close because the councillor is a very busy man and has a charity lunch to go to in ten minutes.

'Well, it's us that keep voting for them,' says Jean as the GOGO Girls walk along the corridor, seething at the lack of support from their elected representatives.

Just before they reach the lift they see hope in the shape of a young woman emerging from her office.

'Scuse me, are you a councillor?' asks Bridget. 'Are you the SDLP?'

'No!' she replies indignantly, as if this should be obvious to any sane person.

'But where are they?' asks Bridget.

'I've no idea,' replies the councillor. 'I'm with the Alliance Party.'

'Oh, you're cross community like us, and you've had a quare surge, so you have, so will you support our campaign to get the peace gate open?' says Patricia.

'Certainly!' she replies. 'Here, let's take a selfie.'

The councillor takes a selfie with the women, types two-hundred-and-eighty characters into her phone and smiles. 'There! I've just tweeted my support to ten thousand followers, hashtag GOGO,' she says proudly.

'Is that it?' asks Jean.

'Those so-called peace walls are an outrage,' says the councillor, 'and I promise you here and now that I will put out posts on all my social media accounts every day until every one of those iniquitous walls comes down.'

'C'mere till I tell you,' says Patricia, 'we're not asking for a tweet, we're asking for support. Will you come to our street party in West Belfast?'

'My Uncle Billy's doin' DJ, councillor,' says Roberta, 'and if you come and support us, I'll get him to play "Congratulations" by Sir Cliff for you and your wee surge, and you can tweeter it as much as you like!'

'Okay, send me a DM and I'll see what I can do,' says the councillor as she scurries along the corridor, answering her phone and declaring, 'Really? OMG! That's an outrage!'

'In my day DMs were boots,' says Jean.

'Where's the SDLP?' asks Patricia.

'So the councillors mentioned there are small grants available for groups like yours,' says the good and equal relations manager as she ushers the women towards the exit.

'What do we have to do?' asks Jean.

'Well, if you want a larger grant, you could apply through the LIG and RIG partnership,' she explains unwisely.

'And if we don't want to go through themuns?' asks Jean.

'Well, then, as long as you have all the governance and policies in place and you're up to date with GDPR, you could apply for up to five hundred pounds,' explains the good and equal relations manager, now moving into automatic pilot.

'What's this GDPR again?' asks Jean.

'Well, it's to make sure you keep your databases of personal details secure and safe.'

'Wha?' asks Roberta.

'But we don't have any databases, love,' says Jean. 'We don't even have a laptop between us.'

'All we have is Patricia's very smart phone and it's not even a MacApple,' adds Roberta.

'But, ladies, you still need a proper policy in place to access a grant from the council. We're running a series of workshops on GDPR over the next few weeks that can help you develop your policy.' The good and equal relations manager accelerates her farewell. 'I'm sorry, ladies, I've a flags committee, a bonfire forum and a review of painted kerbstones to attend. Must dash! It was lovely to meet you all. Bye!'

'But where's the SDLP?' asks Bridget.

The good and equal relations manager disappears, leaving the four women crestfallen at the exit door of the city hall.

Patricia scowls and speeds her wheelchair away. Surrounded by bemused tourists, she swivels around and shouts at the top of her voice towards the grand dome. 'I'd love to tell the whole bloody lot of youse in that city hall that you can stick your GRPDs where the sun don't shine!'

26

The day before the street party, Jean rises early and gets to work bleaching her front step especially for the occasion. To her surprise, Sam arrives mid scrub and offers to help.

'Alright, missus? I couldn't sleep last night, so I got up early to come and give you a wee hand.'

'Och, Sam, son, that's very good of you. We've borrowed the windie cleaner's ladders, so can you help put up the buntin'?'

'Houl your horses, missus, I'm only here early until the bookies open, so no one sees me, and I'm only puttin' up red, white and blue.'

For the past two years Sam has lived by the principle that the more he shames his parents the more he gets back at them, so helping Wee Jean needs to be done on the quiet. The last thing Sam wants to hear is his father telling him he's turning onto the right path.

Roberta arrives with bin bags full of bunting.

'Sorry, it's not Twelfth buntin', son. This party is for everyone,' says Jean. 'The buntin's multicoloured for the street party. Sure, show him, Roberta.'

Roberta pulls out a line of multicoloured bunting.

'Look, Sam, it's all lovely rainbow colours like for the Proud march to the city hall.'

'Fuck!' says Sam, but helps put up the bunting anyway.

'You should see the state of the flat that wee lad lives in on his own,' whispers Roberta. 'I wouldn't keep a dog in it.'

'I know, love. At least he's found something good to do. Would you believe that same wee fella who was slabberin' at us a few weeks ago is helpin' us now? He's not a bad wee lad really, none of them are. It's just this bloody country doesn't give the kids a decent chance,' says Jean.

'Och, Jean,' replies Roberta, 'you see the best in everyone, so you do, like Lorraine Kelly on *GMTV*, but, I'm sorry, love, I wouldn't trust him as far as I could throw him.'

Remarkably, on the other side of the gate a similar miracle is being mirrored. Seamie has agreed to help Bridget put up the multicoloured bunting too. He has mixed feelings about this public contribution to reconciliation and so he wears dark glasses and a baseball cap and looks around constantly to check if anyone has spotted him. Seamie remembers how many times Bridget has been to his house with help from St Vincent de Paul. Now it's his turn to help her out, even if it is for some mad cross-community party.

Bridget arrives with a flask of tea and a few Paris buns and pats Seamie on the back. He says nothing but Bridget knows instinctively that he appreciates the warmth.

Anto tags along, but every time Bridget gives him an instruction he points at her half glasses cheekily and says, 'You shoulda gone to Specsavers, missus!' and Seamie slaps him across the back of the head.

The day before the street party dawns and Jean's kitchen table can barely contain the mountain of tray bakes, rows of plastic platters filled with freshly cut triangular egg and onion sandwiches and a multitude of Himalayan pavlovas. Jean is running late and is a little fraught because she almost forgot her weekly visit to old Mrs Taylor up the street, who refuses to let anyone else trim her toenails. This noble task now complete, Jean is catching up on the preparations for the street party. She is baking scones and putting crockery from the cupboards into boxes while Cliff Richard sings 'Summer Holiday' and 'Living Doll' at high volume on the CD player Trevor and Valerie had bought her for Mother's Day a few years ago. Jean is checking the biscuit tin for the remaining fifteen hundred pounds for the kitchen renovations when the doorbell rings. The caller is Seamie, smiling, wearing work overalls and carrying a sledgehammer and a bag of tools.

'Can you start workin' on it next week, son,' asks Jean, pointing to her ageing cupboards, 'after the street party? All them there oul cupboards need knocked out. Then I need the new ones put in.'

Seamie leans on his sledgehammer, inspects the cupboards and strokes his chin, pretending he knows what to do until he decides to come clean, 'I only know how to knock things down, Jean. No one ever showed me how to build things.'

Jean smiles and pats him on the back sympathetically.

'I could get stuck in nigh if ye want?' he says.

'No, love, you'd only get dust on my pavlovas and I've a lot more packin' away to do,' Jean says cheerfully.

Seamie stares wide-eyed at the pile of food on the kitchen table.

'I used to be a quare wee dinner lady, you know, Seamie. What happened there, love?' asks Jean, pointing to the scar on Seamie's neck.

'Prods!' answers Seamie. 'After the match when I was twelve.'

'I'm sure your mother was distracted when that happened.'

'Well, she's been distracted for years,' he says sadly.

'God love her, it must have been hard when your daddy left.'

'Aye, Jean.'

'Patricia says your granda's face is on one of them big memorials at the end of her Liam's mother's street.'

'Oh, aye, he was a hero for Ireland,' Seamie answers, almost automatically. Then his eyes lower and his voice falls, 'Pity my da wasn't more of a hero,' he says.

Seamie never really knew his father. Mickey McGuigan had abandoned his family years ago. His Uncle Danny said his brother couldn't take his wife's drinking any more, but Seamie thinks this a weak excuse for a man whose father had fought and died for his country. He left without even saying goodbye and has had no contact with Seamie since. Some people say Mickey McGuigan lives in a big house in Liverpool with a new family, but no one knows for certain. Seamie's brothers are older and emigrated to build a new life for themselves in New Jersey, but Seamie is stuck.

'Now, don't be speakin' ill of your daddy, love,' says Jean. 'I'm sure he would have done anything for you and your brothers.'

Seamie thinks for a while. 'Well, he used to take us fishin' when I was wee,' he says, remembering, 'up to the bridge at Toome.'

'There you are!' says Jean.

'We used to try to catch eels up there,' recalls Seamie, visibly brightening for a few moments.

'Och, my Derek use to fish up there before the Troubles,' says Jean. 'I used to hang up his green waders to dry in the backyard.'

'The bastard left us, Jean. That's all that matters now. That's all that will ever matter,' says Seamie.

Then, at just the wrong moment, the doorbell rings and interrupts the conversation. Jean leaves the kitchen to answer the door, still thinking about Seamie's family story. Left alone in the kitchen, Seamie looks around the room examining the pictures of Jean's family on the wall, an old postcard of a bridge in Donegal and a bracelet of brightly coloured beads. 'And nigh on the UTV!' he mocks Julian Simmons to his face on the signed picture postcard pinned below Jean's heroes: Cliff Richard, Prince Harry and Meghan Markle and her grandson Darren. Seamie leafs through a stack of alien reading material consisting of the Belfast *News Letter*, an issue of *The People's Friend* and two thick Catherine Cookson novels. Then he notices an open biscuit tin sitting out on the sideboard.

Jean opens the front door to Sam. He is ready for work, carrying a bag of tools and wearing a pair of old torn jeans with numerous paint stains.

'Did you talk to your doctor about how you've been feelin', son?' she asks.

'Aye, I'm going to see some shrink,' Sam replies, eyes down. 'Doesn't mean I'm mental, like!'

'Och, catch yerself on, son. That head of yours is well and truly screwed on,' says Jean.

Jean returns to the kitchen with Sam, hoping for the best possible interaction with Seamie. The two young men look at each other in recognition, shock and then disgust. They have never been in such close proximity before and certainly not in a domestic setting.

'Fuck!' they say simultaneously.

'Now youse needn't be startin'!' warns Jean. 'Seamie's knockin' out the cupboards and Sam's gonna build the new ones. Youse are my workmen for my new kitchen and I expect youse to work together and do a good job for an oul done woman. Alright?'

'Missus, you're wired up to the moon if you think I'm workin' with him,' says Sam.

'Aye, well I came here to do a job for you, Jean, not to talk to the likes of him!' says Seamie. 'You'll be fuckin' sendin' us on some cross-community holiday to America next!'

'Och, for God's sake,' says Jean, taking both lads by the arm, 'wise up, wee lads! The two of you are just the same, you know. You're decent lads if you'd get off them oul drugs and forget about all that oul sectarian nonsense and get a job and settle down with a nice girl.'

Seamie has had enough of this and turns to walk out of the kitchen, brushing roughly past Sam.

'Hun!' grunts Seamie.

Sam raises a fist and Seamie raises the sledgehammer in response. Sam knocks the sledgehammer out of Seamie's hand

and it lands on the kitchen table knocking over a dozen freshly baked pavlovas.

'Boys – my pavlovas!' shouts Jean.

'Fuck you off back to your own side where you belong!' Sam shouts with all the visceral hatred of several generations. He swings his tool bag and it just misses Seamie's head but knocks Darren's picture off the wall.

'Now look what you've done!' shouts an indignant Jean. 'My wee Darren's a real hero not a bloody ceasefire soldier like youse two!'

The two young men ignore Jean and square up to one another. Seamie punches Sam right in the face. Sam returns a punch to Seamie's stomach, winding him in the process. Seamie grabs Sam around the neck and the two young men wrestle to the floor of the kitchen, toppling the table and all its lovingly prepared contents.

'I hear your ma's an oul wino!' shouts Sam.

'Well, my mate Anto says he shagged your sister in the Waterworks!' retorts Seamie.

Of course this accusation is not true, but Anto thought the boast sounded impressive at the time.

'Wise a bap, wee lad,' says Seamie, 'the only thing he's ever shagged is a sheep up the Black Mountain if he's lucky.'

Seamie tightens his grip around Sam's neck now and spits on him with added ferocity. The two young men are wrestling roughly on the floor of the kitchen, legs and boots flailing in every direction.

'Do you want me to call the PSNI?' shouts Jean.

Seamie's lip is bleeding and as the fight becomes more intense Jean attempts but fails to position herself in between the two young men.

'Only good Taig is a dead Taig!' spits Sam.

'Orange bastard!' Seamie retorts.

'Stop that dirty talk in my kitchen and get up and behave yourselves!' shouts Jean.

But this is more serious than the many fights Jean broke up in the school dinner hall. Eventually she gives up on her usual tactics and decides to try a different strategy. Jean takes her full bulk and sits herself down heavily on top of the two brawling teenagers. The shock and weight of her physical intervention causes the two young men to stop fighting and look up in disbelief at Jean.

'What the fuck are you doin', missus?' shouts Sam.

'For God's sake, will youse stop fightin'!' she pleads breathlessly.

There's a rumble of thunder outside, a flash of lightning and heavy rain hammers the roof of Jean's house. The shock of Jean's intervention and the roar of thunder is enough to distract the two young men and the battle ends as quickly as it had begun. Lying on the floor with a pensioner on top of them, Seamie and Sam look at each other directly for the first time and nod to one another that the battle is over for now. Jean moves aside slowly, holding onto her bad knee, and Sam and Seamie gradually untangle. The erstwhile combatants get up from the floor and dust themselves down removing all traces of pavlova, but still stare at one another menacingly.

Seamie helps Jean back onto her feet.

'Are you alright, Jean?' asks Sam.

Jean does not reply but shakes her head and quickly ushers Seamie out of the kitchen towards the front door. When she closes the door behind him she rests against the doorframe, very out of breath, and rubs her chest.

'Come back next week, Seamie!' she calls through the letterbox, and panting she adds, 'I'll pay you for a good job done. You could buy somethin' nice for your Ann Marie and that wee baby of yours!'

'Forget it, missus!' shouts Seamie from the street as he heads towards the peace gate in the torrential rain. He turns around and with tears of frustration on his cheeks yells at the top of his voice over the sound of the rain and thunder, 'I hate this whole fuckin' shithole!'

Meanwhile Sam is composing himself in the kitchen. He wipes egg and onion from his hair and looks around the room at the pictures of Jean's family on the wall, an old postcard of a bridge in Donegal and a bracelet of brightly coloured beads. Then he notices the open biscuit tin sitting on the sideboard.

A few seconds later Jean returns to the kitchen, still out of breath and holding her chest.

'You wee lads will be the death of me,' she says.

Sam grunts.

'Same goes for you, son, as for him,' she pants as she ushers him out. 'Calm yourself down and come back here next week, after the street party, and get this job done.'

Sam is unrepentant. 'Wise up, missus. You shouldn't have brought one of themuns over here – imagine lettin' a Fenian into your house!' he barks and points aggressively at Jean, 'You need to watch yerself!'

Jean ignores the apparent threat. 'Will ye stop all that oul talk, Sam. I know rightly you don't even mean it. For God's sake, I'm just tryin' to give youse both a chance.'

Sam puts his hands on either side of his head and gives it a shake before pulling up his hood. 'My head's melted, so it is,' he moans as he walks out, slamming the door so hard that Jean jumps.

Jean returns to the kitchen alone still holding her chest. She notices the biscuit tin has been disturbed. She looks inside. It's empty. All the money is gone. She sits down on a chair beside the upturned kitchen table surrounded by pavlova debris and places her head in her hands.

'Och, Seamie,' she cries, shaking her head. 'If you'd asked me, I'd have lent you some of the money. Sure, I was goin' to pay you for the work anyway!' She looks up at her favourite photograph of Derek in his good suit. 'I know, Derek, love. I'm too soft. That's what you always said. But I just wanted to give the wee lad a chance.'

The storm continues outside as Jean starts to tidy the mess and get back to work replacing the damaged desserts. At one point she looks out the window and is certain she sees a thin bolt of lightning strike the top of the peace wall.

'You're gonna have to do better than that, God,' she says.

27

It is five thirty on the morning of the street party. The storm from the night before has cleared and there's a softness in the air. A single magpie is hopping along between the spikes on the top of the peace gate, pecking for insects at the tiny gaps between the jagged tops of the railings. The only sound is the slight reverberation of pecking on steel. In the stillness of the early morning it sounds like the faint echo of an ancient harpsichord.

Both Catholic and Protestant streets are empty when a solitary PSNI Land Rover draws up beside the gate. Despite the peacefulness of the scene, it's one of the old-style grey armoured police vehicles from the Troubles era. A young policewoman jumps out of the passenger side and walks towards the gate. She's one of those new PSNI recruits who looks uncomfortable with a bulletproof vest and a gun.

Jean stands in her nightie peeking through her net curtains, monitoring every move of the young woman as she unchains the gate with a complete absence of ceremony. Another two colleagues get out of the Land Rover and assist her in pushing the huge gate open. It takes some effort for the initial shunt as rust and dirt restrict the action of the unused hinges. But after a sudden screech of steel on steel, which causes Jean to jump in fright – because it brings back her innate response to such sudden noises in the bad old days, the police officers manage to move the hinges and the gate slowly swings open with a yawning metallic wail. The sky does not fall in.

Jean feels a shiver running up her spine. She notices goose pimples on her arms. For the first time the peace gate is open. Jean smiles and returns to her kitchen to catch-up on replacing the destroyed pavlovas.

By nine o'clock there's already a buzz in the street. All the GOGO Girls and many of their friends and neighbours have arrived and are putting the finishing touches to the tables. The gate remains open as if it's normal and the mood in the street is relaxed and happy. Music, colour and vibrancy have replaced dourness and fortification. The only hint that something's awry are the few police officers discreetly present beside the gate.

'Thank God it's not raining, for once,' says Bridget.

'Thank Frank Mitchell,' says Patricia. 'I sent a wee tweet to him yesterday to say he was my favourite weatherman, so he'd better get rid of that bloody storm quick and get the sun out for the GOGO Girls!' Patricia takes out her pink phone and starts to photograph the scene. 'I'm just stickin' these on my Intergam and sending them to Frank before Stephen phones,' she says proudly.

A few seconds later Patricia's phone does indeed ring and she answers immediately. 'Yes, Stephen, this is Patricia reporting live from the West Belfast peace line for the BBC and our gate is finally opened, so it is, and there's no trouble nor nathin' here, so there's nat, and everyone here's on powerful great form ... Yes, Stephen, love, I'll let you get a word in edgeways in a minute ... And there's gonna be face-paintin' and a bouncy castle and tray bakes and all, and I told you, didn't I, that it was safe enough to open this here gate? And I'm tellin' you it's open wide the day, Stephen, and there's no problem and it's all dead on ... And sure half them eejits that phoned you thought it would be World War Three if that gate opened, and I'm tellin' ye here and I'm tellin' ye nigh, to the whole of Norn Iron listenin' to me on the biggest show in the country, all them there peace walls have till come down next!'

While Patricia is broadcasting to the nation, Jean is welcoming more and more people who arrive in the street from both sides of the peace wall. She is genuinely amazed to notice that the drivers on the main road and other pedestrians walking past barely give the newly opened gate more than a few seconds of attention. However, a few passing motorists toot their horns in support and Roberta waves at them and shouts 'Yeoooooo!' It's almost as if it is possible to live beside your neighbours without being separated by a huge steel gate. Jean wonders if there would be the same level of nonchalance if somehow all the peace walls simply disappeared overnight and everyone just got on with their lives without barriers.

By eleven o'clock there are dozens of people of all ages sitting at the two rows of wooden tables across the middle of the street eating assorted party food. There's a sweet party smell in the air, a mix of the odours of diluted orange juice, sugary cake and cocktail sausages. The street is draped in the bright multicoloured bunting and Roberta's deaf Uncle Billy, who does DJ at the British Legion Christmas party, is playing cheerful music through a loudspeaker – a continuous loop of 'Agadoo', 'The Birdie Song', 'The Music Man' and 'The Hokey Cokey'.

'Have you no Daniel nor Cliff?' enquires Roberta.

'Roberta, love, put up or shut up!' responds Uncle Billy as he fiddles with his hearing aid.

'Nightmare!' replies Roberta with a flick of her fringe.

Wee Bertie arrives accompanied by young Dorothy, and as a local hero he receives a special welcome from Uncle Billy.

'Ladies and gentlemen, boys and girls, will you please put your hands together and give a big Shankill—I mean Falls and Shankill, very, very cross-community welcome to the oldest man on the Road. One-hundred-and-two-year-old war hero and great wee man, Bertie!'

Bertie is immaculately dressed, as usual. In fact, he is the only male partygoer wearing a tie. Jean ushers him to his own special seat with an extra cushion at the top of the party table, and neighbours young and old form a queue to ask him to share some of his stories from bygone Belfast. 'Wee Bertie takes extra milk in his tea,' advises Jean, and Bridget provides the necessary sustenance to keep his tales going throughout the day.

At the same time children (some wearing Rangers tops and some wearing Celtic tops) who were born when Wee Bertie hit his nineties are playing together happily and queuing up for the face-painting and bouncy castle. Jean is beaming and enthusiastically serving tea and pavlova while Patricia does the face-painting. She begins by painting Wee Jack's face with black-and-white stripes to advertise the fun. Wee Jack runs around the street barking like a demented miniature zebra, and the promotional campaign proves most effective when the queue of children waiting to be transformed into tigers and lions and clowns soon rivals the queue for the bouncy castle and the refreshments line. A group of students from Queen's University arrives to volunteer their services for the day and Bridget wastes no time assigning them the more manual tasks.

'It's awful good of those sociology students from Queen's to come over here from the Holylands to give us a wee hand,' says Bridget.

'The Holylands?' cries Patricia. 'I hope it's not themuns from the radio and they're not here to get drunk and start a riot. Where are they?'

'It's those boys over there,' says Bridget, pointing towards three young men with long beards, wearing checked shirts, braces and faded jeans. 'They seemed like very nice young people to me.'

'Och, Patricia, love, they're not rioters,' says Roberta. 'That's them hymnsters. All they do is drink swanky coffee and eat funny vegetables you and I've never heard of.'

The harmonious occasion is disturbed only by the arrival of Moanin' Martha.

'That music's too loud and I can't hear myself think in my own house, and have you got permission to block this street, and who's payin' for all this anyway?' she begins.

'Here we go,' says Jean.

'And I hope you haven't invited any of them Syrian refugees here today. We don't want terrorists in our street!'

'Sure, her husband's in the UDA,' says Patricia. 'There's a bloody terrorist in her own bed!'

'Wee Jean's payin' for it from what Big Isobel left her in her will, God love her,' says Roberta, 'so we're not takin' any funding from your husband's precious paramilitary residents' group, so you can dry your lamps, Martha!'

'I hear there are more Roman Catholics than Protestants goin' to that church now,' replies Martha, opening up a new wing of attack, 'and republicans are plannin' to take over the church building, and, oh, my God, they're takin' over everything – the Queen's highway, Stormount, the eleven-plus – and the Protestant people have nathin' left to give!'

'Catch yourself on, Martha,' says Jean and walks away.

'Here, Martha, have a wee Rice Krispie bun and a cup-a-tay and I'll ask my Uncle Billy to put on a wee Willie McCrea song for you, love,' says Roberta.

Martha's voice is finally drowned out by goodwill and she is overwhelmed by offers of freshly baked sweet delights.

While Bridget takes on the role of overall coordinator, Roberta is director of operations in charge of the bouncy castle. She is addressing a queue of excited children, 'Kids, do you wanna come back next week and help me paint a lovely big peace muriel on the wall?'

The throng of children look confused, run past her and invade the bouncy castle. The inflatable monument becomes a chaos of small arms and legs.

'One at a time! One at a time!' Roberta shouts, but is ignored by the revelling children.

'Oh, Jean,' cries Roberta, 'these youngsters are goin' to end up in the Royal for stitches!' Determined to gain some control, Roberta pulls the plug out of the bouncy castle and it immediately starts to deflate with a dozen children still inside.

The collapsing bouncy castle seems to be about to devour several small children as it deflates, but fortunately a serious incident is averted when a flurry of concerned mothers come to the rescue.

'That bloody thing nearly swallowed our Orla, and her with her dyslexia and all!' complains one outraged mother.

'I'll report them oul dolls to health and safety,' threatens a grandmother. 'Our wee Kyle near fell flat on his wee face and he's a very sensitive wee lad, so he is, with his conditions and all!'

Fortunately for the GOGO Girls the newspaper photographer and TV camera crew miss this particular incident as they are focusing on getting the best pictures and most impactful interviews. A tall, silver-haired English TV journalist is interviewing street party attendees. After years of reporting on much more newsworthy events on these streets, he believes firmly that these people will always need to be separated by walls, but it's a quiet news day, so needs must.

Seamie and Anto are standing with hands in pockets on the street corner across the road, observing and intermittently kicking the red-bricked gable wall and spitting on the kerbstones. They want to communicate that they are present but not attending the street party. Across the road and further up Jean's street, Sam and Lee are sitting smoking seriously in a stolen Vauxhall Astra watching the street party with narrowed eyes over lowered baseball caps. The two pairs of lads can see each other clearly enough to ensure the other side can detect their aggression.

'I don't know what the fuck we're doin' here, Seamie,' whines Anto. 'I could be playin' Assassin's Creed on my PlayStation instead of watchin' this crap!'

'Wise up, wee lad,' replies Seamie. 'It'll be interestin' to see what happens, and sure them oul dolls are all smiles for once.'

'Well, I'm goin' as soon as I get my stuff from the poke man,' says Anto.

Anto never uses the drugs he buys when he queues up at the ice cream van with Seamie. He doesn't like the way they make him feel and he sells them on at school in case his mother finds them.

'Sure, he's not even here yet,' says Seamie. 'He has to supply half of Poleglass before he comes anywhere near here.'

'Look who is here, though,' says Anto, pointing to Ann Marie arriving with the pram along with her mother and a few neighbours.

Seamie sniffs, 'Aye, so what?'

'She's bringin' your wain over there to mix with wee Prods, Seamie. What are you goin' to do about that?'

'Anto, I think wee Prods shit their nappies and gurn their lamps out the same as our babies, you know.'

'Aye, but you don't want your kid to marry one, do you?'

'Anto, son, will you fuck up. No babies are gettin' married here the day.'

The journalist asks Jean and Patricia for an interview and the two women agree – Jean reluctantly and Patricia enthusiastically. The journalist fails to stifle a cynical sigh as Patricia asks for a few minutes to apply fresh pink lipstick and check her hair.

'People from both sides of the community seem to be having a very good time here today,' begins the journalist in his broadcasting voice. 'Why have you organised this street party?'

'Well,' replies Jean, 'the pensioners round here believe it's about time we started to think about taking these peace walls down and—'

Patricia interrupts, looking straight into the camera, 'As I told my good friend Stephen Nolan on the radio this morning, these walls just keep the young ones hatin'!' Patricia holds a smile looking into the camera lens and fluttering her eyelashes.

'Some people would say you are being very idealistic – that these walls will never come down,' continues the journalist.

Jean has an immediate response because she knew this was

bound to be a question, 'Well, we did a wee survey and most people on both sides said they wanted this gate open during the day—'

'Her best friend couldn't even get round the corner when she died, ya know,' interrupts Patricia again.

The journalist nods patronisingly, clearly confused by the remark, but it will be edited out anyway, he thinks, as he notices Wee Jack tugging at his trouser leg. 'And as a victim of the Troubles, you are still prepared to see these barriers being broken down?' he asks Patricia, eyeing her wheelchair.

'Listen to me, son, I'm no victim of nobody – I'm a survivor!' announces Patricia.

'Aye, she's like Beyoncé!' shouts Roberta as she passes by chasing a small crowd of bouncy-castle absconders.

Sam and Lee are arguing now in the stolen Vauxhall Astra.

'I don't know what's wrong with you the day, wee lad!' complains Lee.

'None of your fuckin' business!' snarls Sam.

'If you wanted to nick that wee yella Mini, you should've took it instead of this bloody jalopy!'

'Fuck off, dickhead!' shouts Sam, slapping Lee roughly on the back of the head.

Lee has had enough and he jumps out of the car to make his own fun. He runs across the road and stands behind the TV journalist making obscene gestures towards the camera from the background. The journalist has been here before and makes a *cut* sign across his throat in the direction of the cameraman.

Lee misunderstands this as a direct threat to him for his interruption. 'I'd love to see you try it, ya big fruit!' he shouts at the journalist.

After several more obscene words and gestures are exchanged between the youth and the journalist, some order is restored and the interview continues.

'But some will say that people in areas like this simply don't want the walls to come down. They say you could never live together,' he says, thinly masking his own opinion.

Jean picks up the inference immediately. 'Well, they don't live round here,' she responds. 'Look at this! Protestants and Catholics and even wee Poles and whatevers all havin' a good day and workin' together. This is the future for Belfast, so it is.'

Patricia gives another exaggerated nod to the camera as the journalist looks down with confusion at the incongruent image of a pygmy zebra pulling at his trouser leg. The interview comes to an inconclusive end when the infamous ice cream van appears and slowly creeps towards the street party. Bridget spots the alien vehicle immediately and gestures at Jean to join her. The two women walk towards the front of the ice cream van as it begins to drive towards the crowd. To the partygoers surprise the two old women start to shoo away the ice cream van. Some people are confused at this apparent hostility towards the poke man as everyone else has been made so very welcome here today and a double ninety-nine and an oyster shell would be added extras for everyone to enjoy. Then Roberta and Patricia begin to whisper the truth about the ice cream van among the uninformed revellers.

'Yer man there in that van comes here every week to sell the youngsters drugs, nat pokes!' shouts Wee Bertie with a wobbly wave of his walking stick.

Within a few minutes other people join Bridget and Jean at the end of the street in shooing the ice cream van away. It's a remarkable scene. Never in the history of West Belfast has a poke van been so unwelcome. Eventually the undesirable vehicle turns around aggressively and starts to drive off with a squeal of tyres and a defiant ring of its chimes.

As the van moves off, Patricia manoeuvres her wheelchair into the middle of the road to ensure the fleeing drug dealer can see her in his rear-view mirror. She raises her fist and while filming herself on her pink phone shouts at the top of her voice in the direction of the departing van, 'Up yer hole with a big jam roll!'

The street party applauds this act of defiance and the celebrations continue apace. Around one hundred people of all ages from both sides of the wall enjoy the activities and the rain stays away – along with Big Stan and Wee Malachy. Lee sheepishly rejoins Sam in the stolen car and they depart for a road trip to the amusements in Millisle in the Vauxhall Astra. Seamie and Anto go in search of the ice cream van. Then, as three o'clock approaches, Jean disappears into her house for a few minutes to collect her notes and her thoughts for her speech.

'Jean's doin' her speech at thee like the Queen,' boasts Roberta.

At five minutes to three Bridget stands up and raises her hands to the assembled crowds of families now seated on benches at long tables the length of the street.

'Turn that bloody racket down, Billy!' shouts Roberta to her Uncle Billy, and he turns off 'Simon Says' in mid verse.

The noise of the crowd slowly dies to a quiet scoffing of egg and onion sandwiches and an occasional cry of a baby. Billy hands Jean a microphone as she stands on her front step to address the crowd. She takes a deep breath and notices that her handwritten notes are shaking – her hand has a more pronounced shake today than the one that has developed in recent years.

Okay, Derek, love, she thinks, here we go! 'Hello, everyone. My name's Jean Beattie and I've lived in this street all my life. I grew up here before that peace wall went up. I swung on them lampposts and I courted wee lads up that entry. I've bleached this front step more times than I can remember. I started and ended my married life here and I brought up my wee son here.

'I'll never forget the day they put that gate up. Nearly everyone demanded it! In all them years I've known that the people on the other side were ordinary families just like mine. They may have wanted a different man to rule them but I never doubted that they had the same problems as our side and wanted nothin' but the best for their childer too. And no matter what our leaders said about them or their leaders said about us, no matter how many terrible things we did to each other for the sake of some bloody country, I knew in my heart that we were neighbours. We were neighbours before the walls went up, we were still neighbours even when our men were killin' each other, we're all sittin' here today as neighbours, and we'll be neighbours again when that wall comes down for good—'

To her surprise, Jean is interrupted by a warm and lengthy round of applause.

'Go on, ya girl ye!' shouts an elderly man with a cocker spaniel and one remaining buck tooth.

'Get her up to Stormount nigh!' cries a young mother with her twins on her knees, snatter tracks tripping them.

'Oh, my God!' cheers an excited Roberta. 'Our Jean's givin' a speech like she's Angela Miracle at the Unified Nations!'

The applause dies down and Jean fixes her hair and takes another deep breath. Her hands have reverted to her normal shake. 'I don't know about yousens, but I'm fed up seein' buses and black taxis carryin' loads of tourists from all over the world, comin' up here from their swanky hotels in the town, to see this bloody wall as if it's something brilliant.'

'Aye,' shouts Roberta, 'them Americans are more interested in takin' a black taxi to that friggin' wall than seein' where they built the *Titanic* and or even where they made that Gay Man's Thrones!'

'They get out of their coaches for five minutes,' Jean continues, 'they write their names on the peace wall or some oul nonsense by Yoko Ono, take photos to show all their friends back home how divided the eejits in Belfast are and then they go back to their nice hotels without spendin' so much as ten pence over here.'

'Blinkin' disgrace!' shouts Patricia.

The mini zebra on her knee barks.

'A few weeks ago we met two very wise women from

Rwanda at our peace wall. They came all the way from Africa to tell us how they had survived the genocide. They told us we could never really claim to have peace in Belfast while that wall remains. One of them asked us a very hard question that she has to ask herself every day when she sees the neighbours who killed her family out of prison and free – "How can I reconcile evil and forgiveness?" But she has chosen forgiveness as the only way to survive after violence. Forgiveness ... not walls.'

A hush descends on the crowd as many people wipe tears from their eyes.

'So why don't we take the walls in our minds down right now? What are we waiting for? Then we can take this hateful wall down brick by brick and build a museum and a hotel and a restaurant and a wee shop for souvenirs like everywhere else in the world that tourists go. Why can't they bring some jobs for the youngsters who live round here to give them a bloody chance so they don't end up joyridin' and riotin'? Why can't we help the youngsters build bridges and not walls like we did?'

The crowd cheers again.

'And before I forget, I want to thank everyone who helped make today a big success – Bridget and Roberta, and Patricia from *The Nolan Show*, and everyone else who made buns and sandwiches, and Billy for the microphone and the music, and Seamie and Sam for helpin' with the bunting – they're not bad wee lads, you know.'

Roberta stands up. 'And thanks to Wee Jean, our leader, who has the heart of a lion!'

The crowd applauds and Jean flushes.

She continues, 'If they built a hotel up here, there'd be loads of jobs. I'd even come out of retirement and help them with the dinners. Bridget there would help in an emergency if some Chinese woman was havin' a wee baby! And our Patricia's Liam would take the Germans on a wee tour of all the bookies shops on the Falls Road!'

The street releases a cross-community laugh.

'So, anyway, I'm not gonna stand here all day slabberin' like some gabshite on Nolan.' Patricia looks slightly offended. 'I just want to say one last thing. In our wee survey, seventy-eight per cent of the people in this community, and I mean the whole community on both sides of this hateful wall, seventy-eight per cent said they wanted this gate opened during the day, and so we are here today to tell all the people who are paid very well to make our community a better place – the MLAs, the councillors, the community representatives—'

'Aye, LIG and friggin' RIG!' shouts Patricia.

'And the clergymen and the funders and the PSNI and the whole bloody lotta them that we want this gate open!'

'Get Our Gate Open!' shouts Patricia.

As Jean sits down and pours a hasty cup of tea to calm her nerves, everyone else stands up in a stirring ovation. Roberta stands on one of the tables, squashing an unfortunate pavlova underfoot, and leads the whole street party in a chant of 'GET OUR GATE OPEN, GET OUR GATE OPEN …'

Patricia starts her own chant, 'What do we want?'

'THE GATE OPEN!'

'When do we want it?'

'NIGH!'

The cheering and chanting only subsides when Roberta's Uncle Billy resumes pumping music through the loudspeakers with 'Something Inside So Strong'. Patricia leads the crowd in a sing-along of the chorus, 'There's something inside dead strong, so there is, I know that I can make it, though you're doing me wrong dead wrong, so you are …'

As the music finally fades Patricia attempts to continue her performance with an acapella rendition of 'We Shall Overturn' but it's clouding over and it's getting cold now, so the crowd decides it's time to wrap up. She finishes one final embarrassing rendition of the song alone and finishes with a polite round of applause from the GOGO Girls at the end.

As the clear sky darkens people start to say their thank yous and farewells and exchange cross-community hugs and handshakes with old neighbours they haven't seen in years. Many of the residents approach the GOGO Girls to shake their hands and give them words of support and encouragement.

'Don't youse be givin' up now,' advises Sheelagh, Bridget's next-door neighbour. 'All the people round here are right behind you, especially the ones who never get a chance to speak up, so youse keep goin'. Youse are doin' a great job!'

Of course there are a few begrudgers in the crowd who feel compelled to offer their critique.

'I noticed the ones from the other side got more plates of tray bakes on their tables than the Protestant people,' says Moanin' Martha harrumphing, 'and not one child from this side was offered a Tayto Cheese and Onion sandwich!'

Wee Bertie approaches Jean for a quiet word. 'Well done, Jean, love,' he says. 'I never wanted this wall, even in the worst of times. I always thought it benefited others more than it helped the good people round here. Remember that bridge in Donegal on the postcard I gave you nigh, Jean, won't you?'

'Of course I will, Bertie. I'll keep it till the day I die, love.'

'Nearly a thousand years old that bridge. The bridges you're building could last longer than that – certainly longer than I'm going to last!'

'Och, Bertie, you're a great wee man,' says Jean, and hugs Bertie before he hobbles off slowly on his blackthorn stick holding Dorothy's hand.

Liam and Uncle Billy lead a team of men in removing the tables and chairs, and everyone helps tidy the rubbish into bin bags and carry the dishes into Jean's kitchen. By dusk, Jean, Patricia, Roberta and Bridget, along with an odd-looking pygmy zebra on Patricia's lap, are alone on one remaining table in the middle of the street. All that remains of the party is the bunting, the table of four elderly women in the middle of the street and the open gate.

'I'll clear up all them dishes in the mornin',' says Jean.

'I'll come round in the mornin' and give you a wee hand,' says Bridget.

'Hopefully we can persuade Sam and Seamie to stop their oul fightin' and come back to take the buntin' down. You never know, it might be a chance for them to become friends,' says Jean. 'I think they'd like each other if they gave it a chance.'

'God love them, they don't know any better,' says Bridget.

'Well, I need to have a word with Seamie first,' says Jean. 'He has somethin' belongin' to me.'

Jean does not elaborate and the other women do not follow up on her concern. Jean is convinced that Seamie has taken the money from her biscuit tin and with a little reflection, persuasion and common sense will give it back to her soon. As the women look back on the day, Patricia produces a small flask from a secret compartment in her wheelchair and pours a top-up of whiskey into the women's latest cups of tea.

'Oh, now you're talkin',' laughs Jean.

'Liam'll never miss this the night,' says Patricia. 'His back's killin' him with all the carryin' the day and he's away to bed with The Player Channel.'

'Och, sure, he's not a bad oul crater, Patricia,' says Roberta.

'I know, love. Sure, I'd be lost without him,' confides Patricia.

'Well, the only thing missing today for me was my Derek,' says Jean sadly.

'I'm sure he was looking down from heaven and cheering you on the day, Jean,' says Bridget. 'He would have been so proud of you.'

'Aye, him and your Gerard,' says Jean. 'That's if Catholics and Protestants are allowed to sit on the same wee cloud up there with no peace wall down the middle!'

'I'm knackered,' says Patricia, setting down her pink phone. 'My battery's bluttered. I've never Instergrammed and Twittered and BakeBooked as much in one day in my whole life!'

'I know. I got a text from her Valerie sayin' the wee video of you shoutin' "Up yer hole with a big jam roll!" after the poke van has gone venereal!' says Roberta.

'But we've done our best, haven't we?' asks Jean.

'We've done what we can,' says Bridget.

'We're makin' a wee difference,' says Patricia.

'We've done our best,' repeats Jean. 'You know, girls, this day will stay with me as a special day for the rest of my life.'

'Och, Jean, that's lovely,' says Roberta starting to weep.

Jean continues, 'I'm so proud of you all. I will always remember that this was the day when the ordinary weemin of West Belfast stood up – I mean you too, Patricia, love – stood up and said once and for all that we don't want to be divided any more by walls and gates and fences and politicians and churches and community bloody representatives nor nathin'!'

'Here's to the GOGO Girls!' says Roberta, and the four women raise their plastic cups of tea and whiskey.

'CHEERS!'

At five to nine the police arrive at the end of the street. It's getting cold now and the four women turn towards the gate. Roberta, Jean and Bridget stand up and the GOGO Girls link arms as the police officers pull the gate towards them. Once again the rusty steel hinges let out an inhuman wail as the gate moves. Sitting up on Patricia's knee, watching every move, hearing every sound, Wee Jack Surgeoner suddenly howls along with the squealing gate as if joining in some primeval lament. As the opening at the end of the street narrows, one of the policewomen salutes the observing women before the gate is finally and firmly shut once more with a heavy jolt.

The slamming of the gate brings to an end a remarkable day for the brave women of West Belfast.

28

Jean feels exhausted when she finally locks her front door and retires to the kitchen where the table is piled with dishes from the street party. She stares at Wee Bertie's postcard of the oldest bridge in Ireland and contemplates how long it will take for the gate to be opened and removed and for all the peace walls to be torn down forever. She sighs and smiles as she imagines a future in her beloved city where building bridges replaces maintaining walls. She sits down and puts her feet up on her purple leather pouffe.

As she rests for a while she fiddles with the coloured beads on her Rwandan bracelet and prays for forgiveness and reconciliation to bring true peace to her land. 'Dear God, I'm sittin' here like Bridget with her rosary beads!' she chuckles to herself.

She decides she can't look at the dishes any more and is going to make a start tonight, but before she does she takes a few minutes for one of her wee chats with Derek. 'I think you would have been proud of me today, Derek, love,' she says. 'Remember that time them paramilitary gabshites said they were going to shoot you for startin' the wee cross-community football team and you had to hide in your Uncle Roy's caravan in Ballyferris until Big Stan sorted it out? You always told me after that to keep ma head down in this bloody place. Well, love, I did something I'm proud of today. I've kept my head down for the last time. It's different now, you know. The paramilitaries allow us to do cross community nigh, especially if they get money for it. They're even at it themselves! You should see Big Stan and Wee Malachy from the other side – they're as thick as thieves! You were ahead of your time, Derek, love. You were a good man when we needed more good men. No one had to pay you to make peace.'

Despite her tiredness, Jean instinctively gets up and sets about tackling the dishes, and as she stands at the kitchen window she notices that bloody magpie again at the bins. No sooner has she washed the first sticky pavlova plate than the phone rings.

'Hello?' answers Jean. 'Hello, Trevor, son … What, love?'

She glances at the empty biscuit tin.

'Yes, love, I'm tellin' you, it couldn't have gone any better if Julian Simmons himself had turned up. I'm tellin' you, Trevor, things are gettin' better over here all the time. When you and Valerie move back you'll have no regrets, I'm tellin' you, son.'

Then Trevor asks a question that requires a careful answer. Jean eyes the empty biscuit tin again.

'Och, sure, I haven't time for doin' up this oul kitchen, love. It's not about the money. Sure, think of all the mess and hassle, and, sure, it'll do me my day … But wait till I tell you more about the day we've had over here. We got the peace gate open for the whole day. The police only shut it a couple of minutes ago … And we had a brilliant street party and everyone had a great time and people were sayin' it's about time all them walls started to come down, and I'm tellin' you, son, this is the start of something. People are sick and tired of all that oul nonsense that keeps us apart. Change is comin', love. I can feel it in my waters.'

Jean continues to wash the dishes and tidy up one-handed as she speaks excitedly on the phone. 'Yes, love, and your wee mammy was on the TV and everything, although my hair was in a state, but I'm tellin' you, love, I think it's gonna make a difference, no matter what your Valerie thinks, just you wait and see … Your daddy always told me to keep ma head down, but it just goes to show what you can do if you stand up to the bullies … Isn't that what I always said to you when you were at school? Aye, son, it's gettin' better here all the time … Sure, you know, son, deep down you know, no matter what your Valerie says, there's no better place in the world to live than in our wee Norn Iron.'

Suddenly Jean stops cleaning. She senses something is not right. From the corner of her eye she thinks she sees the magpie flapping its wings in her backyard. She tries to put the slight feeling of panic to the back of her mind and continue on the phone.

'Ach, no, love! Sure, I'll talk to Valerie the marra if her head's bad again the night. Sure, when youse two are over at Christmas I'll take you to look at houses in Newtownards, and then youse can come home for good, and then when our Darren – my wee hero – comes back home from Afghanistan, sure, he'll meet a lovely wee Belfast girl and I'll have great-grandchildren to enjoy on my own doorstep, and I'll take them round to the swings in Woodvale Park where I used to take you when you were a wee boy—'

Without warning a petrol bomb crashes through the kitchen window. The flaming weapon lands on the kitchen table and shards of glass fall into the wash-hand basin, stabbing the suds on top of the dishes. Jean freezes. The tablecloth catches fire instantly. Jean screams, falls back and drops the phone. The smoke catches Jean's throat and she stumbles to the floor. The smoke alarm is beeping urgently. Jean can still hear Trevor's tinny voice from the distant earpiece.

'Mammy, are you there? Are you alright? Mammy? Mammy, what's wrong? Oh, my God …Valerie, Valerie!'

The phone goes dead as Jean lies on the floor helplessly clutching at her chest. Flames and smoke fill the kitchen. Jean looks up through the smoke at the pictures of her family on the kitchen wall. Her chest feels very heavy and tight. The pain in her arm is unbearable. She cannot get up and the smoke is choking her. She feels panic but is unable to move. She wants to fight but the pain is too much. All at once she feels so very much older than she has ever felt. Jean is so very, very tired. She looks up at the photographs of Trevor and Darren, and into the eyes of her Derek.

Maybe, it's time, she thinks. She begins to feel a calm from within that is stronger than the pain. Maybe, it's time to let go, she thinks. Jean feels so weak, so very weak, but in between coughs and gasps for breath, now there is a smile on her face. I always loved you, Derek, she thinks. You were my man, my one and only. I'll see you soon, my love. My Derek. Jean's hands are clasped together as if in prayer, and she touches her Rwandan bracelet. She feels a deep, deep peace.

Somewhere in the smoke-filled kitchen her mobile phone begins to ring again as Trevor desperately attempts to reconnect with his mother.

'*Congratulations and jubilations, I want the world to know I'm happy as can be.*'

The phone seems to mock the tragedy of the situation.

'*Congratulations and jubilations, I want the world to know I'm happy as can be.*'

The song continues as the smoke engulfs the room and darkness pervades.

Finally the music stops.

29

A small woman is weeping in a street in West Belfast. This is a place where many small women have wept before.

Roberta is heartbroken. 'Nightmare!' she cries.

She stands besides Patricia and Bridget in front of Jean's house. She clutches in her hand the postcard of the oldest bridge in Ireland that miraculously survived the fire in Jean's kitchen, but the smell of smoke on the sooty card breaks Roberta's heart.

'She wanted us to build bridges,' she sobs.

'We must be strong for Jean and her family, love,' says Bridget, gripping Roberta's hand like a kindly mother taking the tiny hand of a fretting child.

A tall, bald man smartly dressed is standing on Jean's freshly bleached front step alongside his wife, a very thin blonde woman dressed elegantly in black and wearing dark glasses. They are accompanied by a well built and handsome young man in army uniform.

'She would be so proud to see you all home here today, Trevor, love,' whispers Bridget.

'Sorry for your loss, Trevor. Hello, Valerie, how's your head? I'm awful sorry, Wee Darren,' says Patricia respectfully, trying her best to hold her emotions together.

Jean's family bend down to envelope Patricia with a loving hug.

A crowd of neighbours from both sides of the peace wall are also gathered outside Jean's house to join her family and friends on this, the day of her funeral. Many of the same people were here for the street party only a few days ago. On the wet pavement outside the house is a small collection of flowers and wreaths from family and friends, including a huge wreath sent jointly from LIG and RIG. Big Stan and Wee Malachy had organised a facilitated dialogue in the Europa Hotel the day after the attack and agreed it was better not to attend the funeral, but that a wreath would be an appropriate public indication of their condolences – and also it would help with the underspend on their Peace grant.

As friends and neighbours shake hands with the bereaved family, the multicoloured bunting still flies forlornly above the street, not just because no one has had the will or energy to remove it, but because the men who put it up are wary of becoming the next target.

Trevor and Darren are thanking people and nodding stoically when the Bilton brothers begin to anxiously carry the coffin out of the front door of the smoke-damaged house towards the single black hearse parked outside. The kitchen was destroyed but the fire fighters had saved the rest of the house and Trevor had insisted that his mother's coffin rest in her home. Roberta takes hold of Darren's hand. She is inconsolable. Bridget takes Patricia's hand.

'Are you alright nigh, Bridget?' asks Patricia. 'It's a mercy the one they put through your windie landed in your dishes.'

Bridget nods quietly. She seems very frail. Today she misses Gerard more than ever. More than on the day he died. Today is one of those days when she feels she has lived too long. 'Remember what Grace from Rwanda said about how she was supposed to be wiped from this earth. Well, for some reason I am still here too,' she says.

Bridget is shaken but clearly not broken.

'If that bloody gate had been open, the ambulance might have got to her in time. Only half an hour earlier and the gate *was* open. A heart attack doesn't have to be fatal if they get to you on time,' says Patricia.

'The wall killed her,' says Bridget.

'Some cowardly wee bastard killed her,' says Patricia, 'but that bloody wall will be the death of all of us.'

The undertakers carry Jean's coffin towards the small pedestrian opening in the peace wall beside the huge locked security gate across the road at the end of the street. Jean passed through this space thousands of times. The Bilton brothers, still recovering from the drama of Big Isobel's funeral, are feeling a dreadful sense of déjà vu.

'God love her,' sobs Roberta. 'They wouldn't even open the gate for our Wee Jean today ... and that's ... that's what she died for!'

'Security considerations, my arse!' says Patricia.

The undertakers stop at the pedestrian opening and the mourners take their places behind the coffin. Two magpies sit on top of either side of the gate, as if forming a guard of honour.

'She wanted to be driven round the corner in a big black hearse with us all walking behind her,' weeps Bridget.

'Like ... like Lady Di!' sobs Roberta.

The Bilton brothers embark on an attempt to carry the coffin through the pedestrian opening, with little confidence based on recent experience. Young William and Young Mervyn have a look of fear on their faces. However, to everyone's surprise, due to Jean's small stature, the coffin just squeezes through the space.

'Well, at least she fits through, God love her,' says Patricia with a sad sigh of relief.

The rest of the mourners sombrely file through the pedestrian opening for the two-minute walk to the church around the corner. A PSNI Land Rover is parked across the road at a respectful but watchful distance. Neighbours from both sides of the peace wall stand quietly on either side of the road, some of them holding hands. It truly is a sorry scene.

'Darren says we're takin' her up to the Roselawn cematorium after this,' weeps Roberta. 'I just gave him her favourite Cliff Richard CD because Wee Jean always told me she wanted to go down into that there big oven with Sir Cliff doin' 'From a Distance'.'

30

The crowd disperses and the small congregation of mourners take their seats inside the smoke-damaged church. Outside there is silence in the empty streets but inside the church is full of grief.

'Will we ever get the smell of smoke away off us for good?' asks Patricia.

'We had thirty years of bombs and then Primark and now all this – nightmare!' weeps Roberta.

There are whispers across the pews speculating on the identity and motivation of the murderers. Wee hoods? Paramilitaries? Drug dealers? No one is prepared to point any fingers directly but it appears as if the same hands that hurled the petrol bomb through the church window a few weeks ago may also have attacked Jean and Bridget's homes in the shadows.

Inside the sad little church today furniture polish and freshly cut lilies, Jean's favourite, sweeten the smoky odour. The mourners are coughing, weeping, shuffling and waiting for the funeral service to commence. Trevor, Valerie and Darren are chief mourners in the front pew. Trevor stares ahead and Darren holds his mother's hand. Behind the family are seated the remaining GOGO Girls; Roberta and Bridget are sharing a pew and Patricia's wheelchair is parked at the end of the row. Hidden from view inside Patricia's expansive handbag is Wee Jack wearing a brand-new black collar from Poundstretcher for the occasion. Patricia leans forwards to speak to Trevor.

'Trevor, love, I asked all the media to say this is a private funeral and to ask for no crowds outside and to promise me they would stay away the day as a mark of respect. They listen to me, you know.'

'Thank you, Patricia, that's very thoughtful of you,' says Trevor. 'Now you look after yourself, won't you?'

The lovely big educated fella from the Good Community Relations Conference is there in his corduroys. He approaches the remaining GOGO Girls and shakes their hands warmly.

'I'm so sorry, ladies. This is a desperately sad day,' he says. 'The women from Rwanda heard the news and sent a message of condolence. Grace and Alice send all their love and prayers. Jean Beattie made a remarkable contribution to building our shared future.'

'Abso-bloody-lutely!' replies Patricia.

The doors at the rear of the church open and the Bilton brothers steadily carry the coffin inside. Darren and Trevor rise and walk to the back of the church to prepare to carry the coffin.

'She had the heart of lion,' says Bridget.

'There's nobody could match our Jean. She was a very brave wee woman. She took no nonsense from no one. And she made the best pavlovas in Ireland!' says Patricia.

'Wee Jean was the proper mammy I never had,' sobs Roberta.

Unexpectedly, Valerie turns around. 'Roberta, love,' she says, 'after all this is over, you come and stay with me and Trevor for a few weeks, won't you?'

Roberta nods meekly.

'Good luck with that!' whispers Patricia with an elbow dig into Bridget's ribs.

As Jean's son and grandson replace Young William and Young Mervyn Bilton at the head of the funeral cortège, the coffin is carried slowly and with the faintest of trembles towards the front of the church. Here, an elderly man with an unconvincing wig and a shaky baritone voice begins to sing 'You Raise Me Up'.

Patricia takes out a huge white handkerchief. 'Oh, my nerves, I can't take any more of this,' she blurts out. 'It's like Geordie Best's funeral all over again!'

A muffled howling begins to emanate from her handbag. Patricia places one hand inside and appears to grip something very tightly but tries to appear both nonchalant and respectful at the same time. She smiles timidly at anyone in the congregation who dares stare in the direction of her whining handbag. Of course, Patricia does not understand what all the fuss is about. Why shouldn't Wee Jack Surgeoner be allowed into church for Wee Jean's funeral? He's one of God's wee creatures too!

As Trevor leans his face against the cold wood of his mother's coffin, in his mind he speaks to Jean. I know you're at peace with Daddy now, but I wish you were still here with us. We were going to move back, Mammy, I promise you. I just needed more time to persuade Valerie.

Darren carries his grandmother's coffin with all the dignity and decorum he has trained for. Three years ago he carried the coffin of his best mate in the regiment, but it is more difficult to stay in control of his feelings right now.

The minister leads the funeral service with genuine grief in his voice and empathetic references and prayers on the great loss being suffered by Trevor, Valerie and Darren and indeed the whole community. He is wise enough to understand that the best tribute to the departed comes not from the likes of him but from someone who knew and loved her. He invites Bridget to say a few words.

'I'm a quiet woman,' Bridget begins. 'I don't often have much to say and what I do say I keep for my dearest friends and family, but Jean Beattie was one of my closest friends and I want the whole world to hear what I have to say about her here today.'

'Jean always said she wanted Bridget to do her urology,' whispers Roberta to Patricia.

'I first met Jean when she was pregnant with Trevor,' continues Bridget, nodding respectfully in Trevor's direction. 'She was a cheery wee button even then, and even though there were complications with the pregnancy, Jean took on every challenge as a battle she was determined to win. She was as tough as nails, you know, but that doesn't mean she was hard-hearted. Jean had a heart like a warm open fire that you just wanted to be near so you could be warmer too. When Derek was forced out and then when Wee Heather was born prematurely and too young to survive, I saw Jean's courage and her spirit of forgiveness and her lack of bitterness shine through. And, oh, do we need more of that spirit in this country today—'

Bridget is surprised to be interrupted by an approving round of applause.

'Yes, and one day that gate will be opened,' she continues, 'and one day those walls will come down, and although Jean will not be here to see it, everyone in this city will remember that Wee Jean Beattie played her part, and gave her life, fighting without a single weapon in her hands, for a better future for the children of Belfast.' Bridget's voice shakes and for a moment it appears she may break down.

'You're doing great, Bridget,' says Patricia, followed by a muffled approving yelp from Wee Jack inside her handbag.

Bridget takes a breath and a sip of water from the glass offered by the minister before continuing, 'And so, here I am today at the front of this church paying tribute to my friend from the other side of the community – although Jean and I always saw it as one community. Yes, here I am today – a Bridget speaking at a Belfast Protestant's funeral.'

A gentle laugh ripples across the surface of the congregation.

'A Catholic and a nationalist from the other side of that despicable wall out there. Here I am today in a Protestant church – I don't know if it's really allowed by my church or this church – but I really don't care any more. I'm here anyway, and I wouldn't want to be anywhere else in the world but here right now to give a eulogy to my dear Protestant, unionist neighbour. My good neighbour. My best neighbour. A devoted wife, a beautiful mother and doting grandmother. A brave campaigner for reconciliation in this divided society. My dear friend, Wee Jean Beattie.'

The congregation rises in spontaneous applause. Bridget smiles, knowing the appreciation is not for her words but for the life of her friend.

Those assembled join in a warm rendition of 'The Lord's My Shepherd' and as the minister pronounces the final benediction the funeral service comes to the closing hymn, one of Jean's favourites. The doors at the rear of the church are opened, once more letting the light in. Wee Jack leaps out of Patricia's handbag and darts outside where he pees on the back wheel of the hearse. Trevor and Darren and the elder Biltons begin to carry the coffin slowly down the aisle towards the waiting hearse as the elderly organist starts to play most of the notes of 'What A Friend We Have in Jesus'.

At the door of the church the diminutive figure of Wee Bertie is standing sniffling and holding onto his blackthorn stick with utter dignity. He is immaculately turned out in his military blazer and tie and wearing his medals for the occasion. As the coffin passes by Bertie salutes with all the vigour and loyalty of a twenty-year-old soldier.

The congregation begin to sing weakly: 'What a friend we have in Jesus, all our sins and griefs to bear …'

Outside, a magpie alights on the ageing peace wall and surveys the empty streets below. She seeks an opening along the brow of the great barrier and pecks hungrily at any tiny gap between the corrugated steel sheets. Thirty feet below the domineering structure the street is silent. It's still too early for bustle. The only sound is muffled hymn singing from the little church.

'What a privilege to carry everything to God in prayer ...'

The magpie ekes out no subsistence but keeps on pecking anyway – even the birds are stubborn in Belfast. But then suddenly she raises her beak, alert to a distant sound, an approaching vibration. Instinctively she ceases her search for insects. Now is a time for vigilance. The bird scans the streets below with a suspicious eye, expecting an imminent threat across the road. Life springs from one of the red-bricked side streets, rupturing the peace. The startled magpie jumps and flaps extended wings to restore balance.

'Bastards!' shouts a young man at the top of his voice, looking upwards.

The magpie freezes and stares down at the possible predator, unaware that a mere bird is not the target of this aggression.

The attacker runs faster and faster towards the solid separation barrier in front of him. Even the heavy sledgehammer he clutches across his heaving chest does not impede his speed. 'Bastards!' he gulders again and again as hot, angry tears stream down his pale cheeks.

The magpie flaps again in a panicky dance across the crest of the peace wall.

As the aggressor gathers momentum he meets no resistance down below.

'Have we trials and temptations?   Is there trouble anywhere?...'

The rain-soaked streets remain deserted for now.

Crying with fury the young man begins to raise the weapon in his hands. 'BASTARDS!' he screams violently, spying his target.

The magpie shits and flees. She leaves an artistic streak of insulting white excrement along the face of the peace wall. The young man is closing in on his victim now. He accelerates his pace and raises the sledgehammer high above his head to unleash maximum force against the enemy. Just as Jean's coffin reaches the open front doors of the church, Seamie strikes the huge steel hinge of the peace gate with his sledgehammer. The impact of iron on steel reverberates along the road and inside the church. The elderly organist jumps with fright, misplays a B-flat for a C and stops playing the hymn altogether. The mourners cease singing, turn around in silence and look towards the church doors.

Seamie is furiously hammering at the hinges of the peace gate. 'BASTARDS!' he screams.

The gate begins to shudder as the hinges loosen slightly.

The startled mourners come rushing out of the church, in a flurry of black clothes and white hair, past the parked hearse in which Jean's coffin now rests, to see what is happening. Their initial fears of another attack are replaced with astonishment at the scene playing out before them.
Bridget immediately recognises Seamie attacking the gate beside the church.

'It's that wee lad Jean tried to help,' says Bridget. 'I don't believe this!'

'Nightmare!' shouts Roberta.

The three surviving GOGO Girls lead the way towards the gate followed by the other mourners. Seamie ignores the gathering audience and continues to hammer at the hinge in a frenzy. Anto runs up the street to the front of the gate, mesmerised by Seamie's actions. He doesn't like seeing Seamie like this. He doesn't want anything bad to happen to Seamie. He can't imagine life without Seamie.

Anto runs up to Bridget. 'Seamie's gone mental, missus!' he shouts. 'He loved that oul doll, so he did. Do somethin', missus, do somethin', please!' Anto points at the scene in front of him in disbelief. 'He's tryin' to do a fuckin' one-man Berlin Wall!'

Wee Jack escapes from Patricia's arms and runs to the peace gate barking furiously, an encouraging sort of bark, at Seamie.

The police officers are emerging from the Land Rover now.

'Girls, we're gonna have to go over to him,' says Bridget. 'He's goin' to get himself arrested and there's no way he's gonna hammer that gate down all on his own.'

'Well, if I had my legs, I'd run over there right now and help him!' exclaims Patricia.

'I'm scared!' cries Roberta. 'I want Wee Jean!'

Roberta is now crying hysterically, as she has many times in the past few days since she heard of the death of her beloved friend. Wee Jack is barking incessantly and jumping up on his hind legs as high as he can as if by doing so he might catch Seamie's eye. The tiny terrier bobs up and down like an angel's yo-yo.

'Seamie, mate, stop it now, seriously, like, mate, you're goin' fuckin' mental, so you are!' shouts Anto with tears now running down his cheeks.

Oblivious to the commotion around him, Seamie continues hammering at the hinges of the peace gate, and although the structure is shaking it shows no sign of opening. Seamie's single purpose is to remove this gate for the sake of Jean, the only person in the past year who was kind to him. His fury and grief blinds him to all around. Ann Marie arrives on the street pushing the pram. The baby is crying loudly. Anto runs over to Ann Marie and grabs her by the sleeve of her pyjamas.

'Ann Marie, you better talk to him. He won't listen to anybody else. His head's completely melted!'

'Seamie!' shouts Ann Marie, trying to sound reassuring rather than panicked, 'look who's here to see her daddy?'

Still Seamie does not look up or stop. 'BASTARDS!' he screams with every blow.

Suddenly, as the police officers talk into their walkie-talkies and discuss when they will intervene, there is an even louder noise.

CRASH!

Like a bomb exploding in a sweetie shop during the Troubles – a huge smashing of steel on steel. The crowd screams with fright. Patricia freezes. Seamie jumps back from the gate wakened from his trance. Slowly the gate begins to topple backwards and forwards, side to side, off its loosened hinges.

There is a painful creaking of steel and a wailing of metal on metal as the structure shakes and wobbles and leans back and falls forwards until finally it succumbs to the forces of gravity. The peace gate falls into the middle of the road with a deafening crash.

For a moment there is silence. Then, as the dust begins to clear, the astonished crowd see Sam Spence jumping out of the driver's seat of the stolen JCB digger he has just crashed into the other side of the gate. He looks over at the crowd proudly and defiantly and gives a finger towards the peace wall. At long last, he thinks to himself, I've done somethin' fuckin' useful!

Then he looks directly at Seamie, who is frozen in the middle of the road with the sledgehammer still in his hands. The two young men hold eye contact and nod slightly at one another. Then Sam simply turns and walks away slowly. As he marches off he leisurely takes one hundred and fifty ten-pound notes from his inside pocket. One note at a time he throws the money backwards over his head as he keeps on walking with his head held high. With every note he releases, he lets go of his shame at stealing Jean's money from the biscuit tin, and each step transforms into a swagger. This is his public penance. Sure, maybe life's worth livin' after all, he thinks. Sam does not look back. The ten-pound notes flutter in the slight wind and land on top of the fallen gate.

Lee arrives on the street and is mesmerised by the scene before him. 'Oh, fuck!' he says quietly to himself and takes out his inhaler for a puff. Instinctively he begins to scurry around picking up as many ten-pound notes as he can lay his hands on and stuffs them into his pockets excitedly.

The hearse, with Jean's coffin inside, drives contemptuously over the remains of the gate and past the abandoned JCB. The police call for reinforcements and begin to cordon off the main road. Ten-pound notes rain down on the bonnet of the hearse like confetti. The mourners follow behind the car, also trampling on the destroyed gate.

As Roberta walks over the top of the gate she stops and turns to the other mourners. She stamps her feet heavily on the former barrier as if she is squashing a huge ugly beetle. 'Well, Wee Jean got what she wanted in the end!' she cries, and stamping her foot and creating a loud bang of steel to accentuate every word she adds, 'She. Got. Our. Gate. Open!'

The crowd stops and a quiet and respectful round of applause breaks out. Bridget, Roberta and Patricia join in. Wee Bertie arrives from the church and once again salutes what he sees. Darren joins him in a salute to his grandmother and Trevor and Valerie embrace. Roberta hopes and prays Jean can hear and see this scene.

When she finally stops stamping, Roberta is sure she can hear Wee Jean whispering in her ear, 'Remember this, girls. If it's the last thing I do, I'll make sure this bloody gate's away for *my* funeral.'

Seamie throws down his sledgehammer, wipes his sweaty, tear-stained face and nose with his sleeve, turns and walks away. Ann Marie, pushing the pram, follows him and catching up puts her arm around him.

'This'll not be the last one of these to come down, girls,' says Patricia. 'Just you wait and see!'

When the last mourner has passed over the felled structure, Wee Jack returns, squats and deposits a perfect steaming turd like a small brown meringue in the middle of the defeated barrier. The three surviving GOGO Girls remain shoulder to shoulder, holding hands, each woman still wearing the colourful Rwandan bracelets they had received just a few weeks ago.

'We must never forget what Grace told us that day at the peace wall,' says Bridget. 'I know in my heart it's what Wee Jean would have wanted. She said, "Every day I must choose to hate or to forgive." Grace told us that even after all she has been through, "Courage takes me by the hand every day and in spite of all the pain, life still offers me smiles."' Bridget turns around and surveys the scene around her. It's an image she thought she would not live to see. She clasps her hands in front of her as if in prayer and says, 'Maybe there is hope for this place after all.'

In a street in West Belfast three women are weeping. This is a place where many women have wept before. But today there are tears of hope mixed with tears of grief because this is the day when the redundant peace walls of Belfast begin to fall down forever.

Epilogue

In 2019 there are more than one hundred gates, walls and fences dividing Catholic and Protestant neighbourhoods in urban districts of Northern Ireland.

After more than twenty years of peace, the areas of Northern Ireland with the most peace walls remain the poorest neighbourhoods with the lowest economic investment, continued paramilitary control, lowest levels of educational attainment and the fewest job opportunities for young people.

The Northern Ireland Assembly says it plans to remove all the peace walls by 2023. By 2019 there has been little significant progress.

Despite the support of millions of pounds from the European Union and the USA, to date only a small number of barriers have been removed through negotiation between community leaders in neighbouring communities.

The Berlin Wall stood for twenty-eight years. The peace walls have divided neighbours in Belfast for more than fifty years.

Talking to the Wall

Still here then?
Dominating my city
Outliving Berlin
Higher than ever
Not stooped with age
Still in charge

Concrete king
We bow to your protection
Under your shadow
Pure segregation
Making us safe
Our ruler

Great steel god
Keeping us all in order
Our side and their side
Titanic rivets
Not rusting here
Still intact

In your youth
We dutifully obeyed
Red bricks in the air
Long-haired kids burnt-out
Blood on the line
Our peace wall!

Sad old fence
Reduced to theme-park status
Stoning just for fun
Black-taxi tourists
When will our minds
Let you go?

TONY MACAULAY

Published 2019
by **so-*it*-is**
www.tonymacaulayauthor.com

The author's right to be identified as author
of this book under the Copyright, Design and
Patents Act has been asserted.

© Tony Macaulay, so-*it*-is, 2019
ISBN 978-1-9161880-0-6
Design by Wendy Dunbar, Dunbar Design
Printed by Martins the Printers Ltd